I0584348

KILLING GAMES

Killing Games, Book One

Reis Asher

A NineStar Press Publication

www.ninestarpress.com

Killing Games

Printed in the USA

ISBN: 978-1-64890-252-9

First Edition, April, 2021

Also available in eBook, ISBN: 978-1-64890-251-2

CONTENT WARNING:

This book contains sexually explicit content, which may
only be suitable for mature readers. Depictions of
graphic violence, murder, suicide, recollections of war,
and PTSD.

Edgar Tobias works as a freelance computer programmer in the city of Anver. Desperate to escape his deceased fathers' fame as a hit singer-songwriter duo, he left the city of Kasyova and the arts behind. He doesn't know he's about to be targeted in a vicious murder game where the prize is a million dollars in cryptocurrency to the first person who can capture his murder on video.

Reis Asher lost everything in the Anverite civil war ten years ago, including their mother. Their father created the agreement known as Unification, which joined Anver and Kasyova to create the Twin City-States of Anver-Kasyova, ending the civil war and ushering in a new era of peace and prosperity.

When they discover the Killing Game, they know that it represents a threat to everything they hold dear and set out to stop it. But powerful forces are at work that refuse to be undermined by one stubborn soul and their sense of justice.

Someone wants Edgar dead, and they'll stop at nothing to see him six feet under... even if that means Reis and other innocent bystanders get caught in the crossfire.

To Jason, for keeping the cats off the keyboard before they could claim co-authorship.

Prologue

"We are live on the site," a deep, smoky, disembodied voice proclaimed.

The camera centered on a circular table. Twelve figures, cast in shadow to obscure their identities, sat around it. In the middle of the table, on a raised dais, stood a gumball machine, numbered balls swirling around inside.

"Before we draw the number, let us lay out the rules for those of you who might be new to the Killing Committee broadcast," the announcer said. "Rule One: the victim detailed in the lottery has been chosen completely at random; any crimes they may have committed are purely coincidental and bear no relevance to the Killing Game."

A harsh, shrill voice chimed in, "In short, we offer no justification or motive for the Hunt besides the thrill of the Hunt. That, and the fame and fortune you will receive when you collect the Prize."

"Two," the announcer continued, "should you commit a crime but fail to achieve the Kill, you will not be protected from law enforcement by this Committee. You will also not be protected for any other victims you kill or maim in the process of acquiring the Kill."

"Fail to do the deed, and you're on your own. Only the Prize will protect you from prosecution for murder. Even then... Only for the chosen target. Think carefully before you strike."

"Three." The deep voice carried a hint of frustration, seemingly at the other person's constant interruption. "The Prize of one million Standard Dollars in cryptocurrency along with legal immunity will only be awarded to an individual or individuals if they can prove, via video evidence uploaded to this website, that they achieved the Kill on the chosen target either directly or indirectly. This video evidence must include footage of the act of murder being carried out."

"Don't even think of trying to fool us. We have eyes everywhere and forgery experts at our disposal. Try to trick us, and you'll find yourself dead... Or worse."

"Those are the rules of the Killing Game," the deep voice concluded. "Commence the drawing."

The balls spun faster and faster within the gumball machine, swirling and twirling. One of the shadowy figures pressed a button and a ball dropped down. The figure grabbed the ball and held it up under a spotlight. The number nineteen was printed on it in black ink.

"Nineteen. Retrieve the file and tell us about the next target." There was some shuffling in the dark room. A manila folder was procured and placed into a pair of silhouetted hands.

"Here are your details about the target: His name is Edgar Tobias, age twenty-nine. He's resided in the city of

Anver since Unification. His address is displayed on the screen, along with his photo. As you can see, he has long brown hair and brown eyes, along with some stubble which may or may not still be present. He is employed as a programmer but recently resigned his tenure at Central Systems to work freelance. He is single, never been married, and has no children. No previous criminal convictions on record. He drives an orange Tempest Nova with a bumper sticker supporting Avon Grey for President."

"Do you, the Committee, authorize the Killing Game to begin with Edgar Tobias as the target?" Murmurs of assent grumbled throughout the room.

A gavel slammed down, the sound echoing off the walls.

"Let the Hunt begin."

Chapter One

EDGAR

Edgar Tobias woke to the irritating beep of his alarm, the three-tone pitch loud enough to rouse even the dead from their slumber. He fumbled for the clock with blurred vision and shut it off before pulling himself up to a sitting position to avoid the temptation of snoozing. He looked at the blinds covering his window, and the lack of light told him it was still dark outside. It was always hard to get out of bed in the darkness, but when he needed to start working early to make ends meet, he had to use all his willpower to make sure he didn't spend all his waking hours beneath the covers.

Thankfully, his computer provided much-needed motivation by choosing that moment to light up, informing him of several unread e-mail messages that might be from his freelance clients. Edgar peeled back the blankets to reveal his naked body and climbed out of bed. He padded across the carpet to his desk. There were a surprising number of new contract offers, given he'd only started freelancing a couple of weeks ago. People wanted mobile applications and they were willing to spend a good amount of cryptocurrency to make their ideas come to life—without having to waste time learning a programming language. Yeah, quitting Central had been the right thing to do. When it became clear his manager wasn't going to allow a promotion unless Edgar went on a date with him, it was obvious the only way for Edgar to restore his self-respect was to quit and go into business for himself.

Sensing a long day ahead of him, Edgar grabbed the bath towel slung over the back of the chair and headed into the bathroom. Cool water always refreshed him, and it had the desired effect—until it became scalding hot without warning. Edgar backed up, uttering a curse. He was covered in lather, and the last thing he wanted to do was call the maintenance manager while he was naked and soaped up... Bad enough Chris always gave him the eye when he came to work on Edgar's aging refrigerator. Edgar suspected his interest was why he'd never received a new one in the building's annual budget. Chris wanted to keep making repairs and inventing excuses to see him.

Edgar shut the water off and walked into the kitchen. He turned on the faucet to find the water was scalding hot there too. Someone had cranked up the water thermostat to beyond safe levels. It seemed like a strange thing to happen, but it could have been a perfectly routine malfunction down in the boiler room. He was a programmer, not a plumber. He poured the hot water into a bowl and added ice from the fridge's ice maker to cool it off. Back in the bathroom, he washed the suds away with the water until he felt clean enough to dry off with a towel. That inconvenience resolved, he dressed in jeans and a T-shirt before dialing the number for the maintenance manager.

"Chris? Yeah. The water's boiling. You might wanna check out the stoker before it explodes... I don't see why you need to come up here for that, but go ahead... Yeah, I'm here right now." Edgar cut the connection, releasing a sigh. Of course, he wanted to make a house call. Edgar hadn't realized Chris was so desperate to see him he'd burn his skin off for a visit, but he could tolerate the guy's presence if it meant the issue got fixed.

Not five minutes later, the apartment echoed with a hollow knock. Edgar closed his e-mails and wandered to the front door. He let Chris in and shut the door behind him. The skinny blond man had been an excellent building manager for years, and despite his annoying swooning over Edgar, he had to admit he liked the fact Chris was friendly, charming, and knew his way around plumbing and heating systems like a pro. While people in Anver often had to deal with slum landlords and half-assed repairs, Chris had always kept his apartment feeling like a luxury pad for half the price a professional usually paid.

"Hey, Chris." Edgar greeted him first, surprised he walked past him without a word. He looked a little pale as he headed to the bathroom and proceeded to throw Edgar's clothes out of the closet so he could get to the pipes.

"Sorry. I probably should have taken care of that, huh?"

"It's no big deal." Chris moved a large box of sweaters out into the hallway. Edgar noticed a clip-on camera on the pocket of his overalls.

He raised an eyebrow. "They're making you wear those for house calls, now?"

"No," Chris said. "I wanted to wear it. The guy down in 2B was creepy as hell last time I was down there."

"I hope you're not wearing it because you think I'm creepy." Edgar took a step back to give Chris some space. "If I've done anything inappropriate over the years, please tell me so I can never do it again."

Chris laughed. "I wish you would do something inappropriate! Why do the good guys have to act like celibate priests? You've got the bad boy look; can't you follow up on that rogue-like charm with a good come-on?" He took a hammer to the one pipe that looked like it was in perfectly good shape, confirming Edgar's suspicions he was here just to see him, as usual.

"I guess I don't do come-ons," Edgar said. "I'm sorry to disappoint."

"I'm not your type," Chris pointed out. "In that we're both bottoms. A tragedy if I may say so myself."

Edgar laughed. "Uh-huh."

Chris stood, the mirth draining from his face. "There. I need to check the stoker in the basement, and you'll be good to go. Want to come check it out with me? I'll need someone to hold the flashlight."

Edgar opened his mouth to say no, he had a lot of work to do, but a hint of something in Chris's eyes made him not want to say no. It wasn't attraction or anything of the sort. Chris seemed sad all of a sudden, as if a black cloud had blotted out the sun. Was he really so smitten with Edgar, or had his ego finally inflated out of control? Regardless, it seemed cruel to make excuses. Especially if that creeper from 2B was hanging around downstairs.

"Okay. Let's go." Edgar followed Chris out of the apartment. They stood in silence as the elevator arrived, and then once again as it descended to the basement level. It chimed, doors opening into a dimly lit passageway. A striplight flickered off and on, struggling to cling to life. A shiver passed down Edgar's spine and he had to fight the sudden urge to leave Chris and go back upstairs. Instead, he forced himself to walk forward until the elevator doors closed behind him.

"Here." Chris pressed a flashlight into his hands, and he turned it on. Green tile covered the walls, a remnant of the building's past as a hospital. After Unification, Anver had found itself with a surplus of hospitals and a shortage of housing. It had made sense to turn some of the towering glass structures into homes. The bomb-proof glass—a remnant of the war—held the heat in nicely.

The huge industrial furnace clanked and groaned as they stepped into the stoker room. Chris looked at the dial and sighed. "Someone's been messing with the heat. I told Kristoff we needed a lock on this door. You know, I love Kasyovans, but it's a pain in the ass when they're too busy with their next show to deal with their obligations."

Edgar vaguely recalled the building's owner saying something about being in a band, but only answered with a grunt. He was ready to get out of here and get back upstairs, where heavy thoughts like loneliness could be buried under a pile of work.

"Hey, Edgar. You ever hear of the Hunt or the Committee?" Chris asked.

"The what or the who?" Edgar narrowed his eyes. "Not a clue what you're talking about, I'm afraid."

"Nothin'. Forget I asked." Chris shrugged.

The flashlight began to flicker in Edgar's hands, throwing them into momentary gloom as the battery signaled its imminent death.

"I think we should hurry up and get out of here," Edgar said.

"Are you afraid of the dark, pretty boy?" Chris mocked.

"Don't call me—" Edgar's complaint was cut off by a force constricting his air supply. It took him a moment of alarm to realize he was being strangled with a rope from behind, its owner pulling back almost hard enough to snap his neck. He swept out with his leg and took his assailant down, grateful for the trick he'd learned in Kasyovan conscripted military service. The rope loosened and he was able to crawl free, gasping for air.

"Shit!" The voice was unmistakably Chris's.

"What...the...fuck!" Edgar yelled, reaching for his throat and coughing until tears swam in his eyes. The rope burn would leave a mark, but if Chris was his assailant, he wasn't safe yet. He fled toward the light, leaving the boiler room and running along the dim corridor. He pushed the instant need for a reason away and concentrated on hammering the call button for the elevator. When it arrived, he entered and immediately hit the close button, aware of Chris racing toward the doors...

They shut completely with a thud and a chime. Edgar slid down the wall, horrified and perplexed, as the elevator ascended. Had Chris tried to *kill* him?

What in the Twin City-States was going *on*?

Chapter Two

REIS

Reis studied the peeling wallpaper of their back room with slight dismay. Their apartment was nothing to be proud of. It was scarred and damaged, just like Reis themself. The civil war had left pockmarks on their soul that had to be borne, even though the residents of the Twin City-States seemed to have forgotten about it.

Reis would never forget seeing their mother die before their eyes, nor the madness that had consumed their father in the days and nights since. He was in an institution now, Alzheimer's forcing him to relive those memories over and over as though he was still fighting on the front lines, even as the nurses fed him Jell-O through a straw.

There was no point even going to see him now. Reis let out a long sigh and rifled through a stack of boxes, uncovering the metal case at the bottom. They picked it up and set it on an aging, weathered desk, clicked open the latches, and lifted the lid to reveal a sniper rifle. It was their father's, a relic of the war that had torn the tiny country in two along ideological and political lines.

Maybe Reis simply didn't want to let go. Maybe they envied the people who had gone back to their regular lives since Unification, mingling with the Kasyovans like they'd always been in the same country, instead of annexed for their own good. Reis couldn't—and didn't—argue against Unification, but there were times when they wondered how the people of Anver had managed to simply forget a period of their history that had once pitted parents against children and lovers against each other. It didn't make sense that a period of such immense loss had been consigned to the history books like it had happened a hundred or more years ago.

Not when the flesh and blood survivors were still drawing breath, entering the prime of their lives with scars that seemed to be ignored. Reis slapped the case closed, suddenly wanting nothing to do with the instrument of death they'd polished, serviced, and cared for in case it was ever needed again. They walked to their weathered piano, took a seat, and lifted the lid to play a few discordant notes. It helped to get those raw feelings out, Reis found. Music was a good way to express things there were no words for, the horror and pain buried deep in their psyche. They fell into a pattern, playing a classic tune from memory: slender, talented fingers pressing down on each key until Reis was satisfied. They'd improved over the years, teaching themself to play more complicated pieces to pass the time. It helped to lose one's mind in the rhythmic patterns of music, to overwhelm the screams and echoes of the past.

The phone rang, tearing Reis back to reality. They'd left their cellphone on the table with the gun case, and they reached now for the sleek, black obsidian tablet that served as Reis's link with the outside world. They brushed their long, chestnut hair back behind their ear and hit the answer button on the screen before they realized the caller ID belonged to a sometime lover they'd not heard from in a while.

"Hey, Ash. What can I help you with?" Reis would rather have forgone the icy formality, but they knew Ash only called when he wanted something. He was long out of favors, and Reis was long past the point where they were willing to indulge Ash out of a sense of guilt.

"I don't know if you *can* help." Ash sounded uncertain—shaken, even—and a pit opened in Reis's gut. They might not have made a good love match, but Ash was still their friend, and the quiver in his voice sounded a lot like fear.

"Just tell me what you need." Reis fought the nausea that always came with their overblown fight-and-flight sense. They wished people would get on with things, instead of beating around the bush. Something bad had clearly happened—the only question was, what?

"Have you ever heard of the Killing Game?" Ash asked.

"Can't say I have. What is it?" Reis perched on the dusty woven grass chair they used in place of a piano stool, resisting the urge to fidget. A fingernail looked appealing, and they battled a losing war to avoid chewing on it. They'd thought that battle against addiction had been won. They'd tossed out cigarettes and grown out their nails into respectable ends with cuticles that didn't look like they'd been through a cheese grater, and they were proud of themself for it.

"It's a site on the Dark Web that's rumored to contract killings via a kind of game. The first person to kill the target detailed in the video and document the murder gets one million in cryptocurrency. I thought it was an urban legend, but the site's real. I tuned in live and now I've got some serious chills..."

"Why are you fucking about on the Dark Web, Ash? I thought you were done with the gambling shit."

"You got me. I—I thought I had it under control, but I was looking for online slots again." An audible sigh echoed down the phone. "But still—I'm really disturbed by this, Reis. The target—he's a guy right here in Anver!"

"This has to be a prank, right? Hang on." Reis wandered into their bedroom where their laptop lay on the bed. They sat down on crumpled covers, lifted the lid, and waited for the display to wake up. They opened their encrypted browser software and navigated into the dark spaces of the Internet, the places few dared to venture. They didn't know why they'd gotten into it in the first place. Maybe because the horror they saw in those underground corners of the Web was the only thing that really made them feel, even if those feelings were terror, rage, and disgust most of the time.

They should have become a cop, and then they'd be able to do something about all this, instead of watching from the sidelines and feeling powerless. Reis's father would have been proud to see them go for a respectable career instead of drifting from one side-gig to the next, never finding a quay to anchor themself to. Reis's love life had been the same way—a string of brief affairs that always seemed to taper out before any lasting connections were made. Maybe that was their fault. Reis had to admit they were commitment-shy.

Reis reached the website, a black splash page with red text on it. They clicked on the button that declared themself in agreement with the terms of service, and a video started to play. The shadowy figures completed their lottery drawing, pulling their number, and Reis wondered if this was just some shady gambling crap after all.

Reis's heart nearly stopped when Edgar's name, photo, and address were displayed. They didn't know the man, but something about his brown eyes, scruffy hair, and roguish smile were charming. They'd expected a syndicate outcast, a well-known criminal on the outs with his former boss—something like that. Not someone so obviously civilian as Edgar. This was no thug who'd gotten on the wrong end of a contract. Edgar was about to be the unwitting victim of a heinous crime. If he wasn't dead already.

"We have to stop this." Reis had almost forgotten they were on the phone with Ash until Ash piped back an answer to Reis's rhetorical statement.

"You're crazy. You can't mess with people like this. They'll kill you!"

"Did you honestly call expecting me to just ignore this?" Reis shut the laptop gently, fighting the roiling cauldron their stomach had become. Unease, disgust, fear—emotions flooded in like they hadn't in a long time. Reis almost welcomed them, grateful for the reminder they were still human, that this life in these rotting walls with the peeling paint wasn't slowly draining their humanity.

"I only wanted to ask if you thought it was a hoax, Reis. This has to be some trolls getting their jimmies off, right? There's no way something like this is real."

"It doesn't have to be real, Ash. Someone just has to believe it is. It only takes one person to buy in and this guy is going to get hurt. If it's only a game—if there's no million in crypto—that's not going to matter if this guy Edgar is six feet under." Reis pulled their knees up to their face, burying their head in the darkness. The world couldn't be this terrible. It couldn't. Despite the civil war, despite world turmoil, black-and-white politics, and all the other struggles the world had been dealing with in recent history, they still believed the human race was, at the end of the day, mostly made up of good people with decent intentions.

The idea some troll—or an organized group—would offer up a person's life at random for their own entertainment destroyed that notion in a heartbeat. Reis felt sick at heart considering it, a horror that constricted their chest, making their binder feel like it might squeeze the air out of their lungs.

"What are you going to do, Reis?"

"I don't know," Reis said. "I think we should get off the phone and you should call the police. If this guy's still alive, he needs police protection."

"Fair enough. Thanks, Reis. We'll catch up later, okay? Don't do anything stupid."

"Likewise," Reis said, and hung up the call. They let out a long sigh, their gut feeling the cops weren't going to do anything meaningful growing by the second. If they dismissed the Killing Game as a prank, Edgar Tobias could die in the meantime. There would be no accountability if he was murdered, and the Killing Game would go on to claim other victims. Edgar would be just another life lost to the ether, another person who slipped through Reis's fingers like so many grains of sand. They'd watched too many close to them die deaths from slow despair in the wake of the civil war, a trend that seemed to baffle officials. Anver, in the wake of Unification, was rich and thriving, but Reis knew it wasn't so easy to erase the ghosts of the past. For some people, the war had never ended. It lived with them every single day, following them around like a shadow that would never release its grasp on their spirits. Some had decided it was too much to go on living with.

Reis opened their laptop and loaded the website again. They watched the cached video, looking for some clue this was a hoax. The video played through to the end and Reis clicked on the site's archives, looking for history. Had the Killing Committee done this before? How did they deal with the "winning" video?

With a chasm of terror widening in their gut, they found what they had hoped to never see: last month's winner. The prize video auto-loaded in their browser. The locale was dark, the footage grainy and shaky, but it was enough to tell the wearer of the body cam was on the hunt. They approached a woman getting into her car and yanked back on her hair, and in one smooth, horrendous motion, sliced her throat ear-to-ear with a knife before she could even scream. They let her body slump to the ground and the footage shut off as the woman choked to death in a pool of her own blood.

Reis vomited, a deep sense of panic gripping their entire being. They struggled for oxygen, realizing they were hyperventilating. Bleak memories flashed before their eyes: scenes from the war long wished forgotten. A child died in their arms, every bone in their body shattered from the shelling of an apartment complex. The schoolhouse, blown to pieces, and the bits of their teacher that had been plastered on the walls. Dad, coming home with his sniper rifle on his back, covered in blood, sitting at the table as though everything was normal. Reis waking in the night, coming out to find Dad sobbing at that same table.

"I've lost my humanity, child," he'd whispered. "Sold it to a cause..."

It was the last time he'd spoken of the war before its abrupt end a few weeks later. Afterwards, it had been like nothing had happened; as if he'd taken those dark years and locked them in a vault, never to be seen or heard from again. Reis had managed their dark memories and panic attacks alone for a long time until they'd broken down at work and ended up seeing a therapist.

The flashbacks passed. Reis found themself lying flat on their back, looking up at the peeling paint hanging down in strips from the ceiling. A draught coming in through the rotting window frames caressed them, making them sway slightly like grass reeds. Reis felt only emptiness where there had been emotion, a void where their horror had sat only moments before.

Yet still something burned inside them, a sense of justice, perhaps, but something that could not be ignored. This Killing Game... It couldn't stand. Not in this vile world or any other. If the cops were unwilling or unable to act, then maybe it fell to Reis to take a stand. They had combat training from their mandatory military service, and they had Dad's sniper rifle, along with a handgun and some knives they'd inherited from his stash. Reis didn't want to kill, but they had the ability to protect this Edgar.

Protect the mark the Killing Committee wanted dead—or die trying. It had to be better than surrendering to hopelessness and despair.

Reis stood up, grabbed a tissue from a box on the nightstand, and cleaned up as best they could. Tying their hair back, they took a deep breath and went to grab their weapons.

Chapter Three

EDGAR

The doors to the elevator chimed as they slid open. Edgar quickly got to his feet, aware of visitors in the building's reception area staring him down for no apparent reason. He pushed past them and out into the vestibule, acutely aware the door to the stairs was on his right-hand side and could come crashing open at any moment.

Chris wouldn't be so brazen as to kill him in broad daylight, with a host of witnesses, would he? So little of this had made sense so far that it seemed impossible to discern his next move. Without any kind of motive, there was no way of knowing the lengths he'd stoop to in order to kill Edgar.

When the door crashed open and Chris came bursting through the opening with a crowbar in his hand, Edgar decided it was best to leave the thinking for later and to concentrate on running. If he could get to his car, he could get out of the city and lie low while he called the building manager and found out what crazy shit Chris was on. Surely, he'd be fired for this insane stunt. Why—

No. No whys. There would be plenty of time for thinking about Chris's reasoning when a strong, healthy young man wasn't gaining ground on his best sprint. He regretted canceling his gym membership as his lungs burned from exertion. He made it to the neighboring parking garage and hid behind a pillar, his body forcing him to take in oxygen. His car was on the third floor. He just had to reach it. Voiceprint activation would unlock it and start it for him, a feature of the latest models he was appreciating now, considering the backup set of keys was still sitting on his computer desk in his apartment.

What a morning this was turning out to be.

Heavy footfalls declared that Chris had vaulted over the low concrete wall into the parking garage and was now stalking the ground floor, searching for any sign of movement like a leopard hunting a gazelle. Edgar glanced toward the concrete steps, realizing now was probably the best chance he was going to get. He broke into a sprint and took the steps two at a time. He didn't even have to look behind him to hear Chris on his tail, the echoes of his squeaking sneakers and soles on concrete loud enough to give them both away.

Edgar yelled as he laid eyes on his car in the distance, practically screaming the codewords to unlock his car and start the engine. The engine turned over, and the car exploded in a fireball that blew the doors clean off, the force knocking both Edgar and Chris to the ground. Edgar scrambled to his feet in a daze, aware Chris was also coming to his senses. He was beyond ready to wake from this nightmare now, to open his eyes and find himself wrapped up in clean sheets. Not here, his face blackened, his lungs aching, with a dull throb pounding in his head where it had hit the concrete. He backed up against the wall, unwilling to accept his brand-new car was nothing more than a twisted husk of burning metal. This wasn't real. This couldn't be happening. It was like something from a movie.

Chris rounded on him, crowbar in his grip and a menacing gleam in his eyes. Edgar slid down the wall he was leaning against, surrendering to his assailant. The only tool left in his arsenal was to try to reason his way out of this. Maybe he could get through to Chris if he could get a word in before the man beat him to death.

"Why are you doing this?" Edgar asked. "I thought—I thought you had a crush on me. If I was wrong, I'm sorry. Look, I'll take you on a date or something. Whatever you want. Just put down the weapon and we'll talk about this like reasonable adults."

"Shut up!" Chris barked, gripping the metal bar until his knuckles turned white. "It's not like I want to do this!"

"Then stop! Whatever I've done, we can work it out, Chris. This is me we're talking about! Lower the crowbar and I won't press charges. I'll even pay for a therapist to help you work through your issues."

"I don't need a therapist!" Chris yelled, his voice tinged with desperation. "I need money!"

"How does killing me get you anything? I'm so confused, Chris. I woke up this morning and suddenly a guy I thought was a friend is trying to murder me. My brand-new car is a fireball. I don't know what I did to deserve this."

"You were chosen by the Killing Committee," Chris explained. "Do you really not know what that is?"

"It's the first time I'm hearing of them. I have no idea what you're talking about, but I'd appreciate it if you filled me in."

"Over a year ago, a site cropped up on the Dark Web. Every month, a group known only as the Killing Committee chooses a victim at random. The first person to send in a video of the victim being killed gets one million dollars in cryptocurrency and immunity from prosecution." Chris wiped the sweat and filth from his forehead. "I couldn't believe the latest one was you. I didn't want it to be true, but I thought I could off you gently and take the money. It wasn't supposed to be this hard... You weren't supposed to fight back. I had the element of surprise."

"Why do you need a million bucks?" Edgar asked.

"My daughter's sick. She's been to doctors in both Anver and Kasyova, but nobody can figure out what's wrong. She's dying, and the only hope I have is to take her out of the country. A foreign doctor has agreed to treat her, but it would cost nearly a million... That's when a friend told me about the Killing Game. She knew how desperate I was. All I had to do was kill you and film it." He slumped, lowering the crowbar. "It's not personal, Ed. I don't want to kill someone I like. But there's nothing I wouldn't sacrifice for my daughter's life. I need you to understand that."

Edgar nodded. "Ditch the weapon and we'll find another way, Chris. *Please*. I'll help you launch the biggest fundraiser you've ever seen."

"There's no other way. I already tried crowdfunding; I earned less than a thousand in pledges." Chris pursed his lips, and Edgar looked on with growing despair as his expression steeled. "I'm sorry. It wasn't supposed to end this way, but if I don't do it, someone else will. Someone with less noble intentions for the money." He raised the crowbar above his head, aiming for a killing blow to the head. Edgar shrank back against the wall, holding his hand up as a shield, waiting for the strike to land that would end his dreams and fulfill Chris's.

The moment seemed to stretch on forever. A distant screech of tires barely registered on Edgar's radar: he wanted this ordeal to end, and quickly. He'd accepted death, though it wasn't what he wanted at all. He'd wanted to see the world. Find a partner to spend his life with. Do something more exciting than write web applications for businesses who abandoned them the next week.

A scuffle ensued, and when the death blow never came, Edgar opened his eyes to see a long-haired stranger tear the crowbar from Chris's hand and throw it aside. Chris threw a left hook at the figure, who ducked deftly into a leg sweep which knocked him off his feet. Chris got up almost immediately. He charged at the stranger and pushed them back into a concrete pillar. Edgar watched as the figure seemed to visibly deflate. He wondered if this third party was some savior, or another bounty hunter out for the price on his head.

God, there was a price on his head. He had no idea how that could have happened. How had he ended up on the radar of this "Killing Committee"? He was the most white-bread, nondescript person he knew; so boring his friends took him along when they needed a designated driver.

He almost laughed at himself as he realized the obvious: the two strangers locked in their duel gave him ample time to get away. He stood up on legs that felt like lead and was embarrassed to note his jeans were wet where he'd urinated in terror. He'd been a coward in the Kasyovan conscripted military, and he was a wimp here too. Fighting wasn't for him. But running—running he could do. With no car to aid in his escape, he started with a sprint to the nearest garage exit. He looked back over his shoulder to watch the stranger incapacitate Chris with a chop to the neck. He slumped to the ground like a sack of potatoes. The figure bent down and checked his pulse before calling out to Edgar.

"You can stop running, now. I'm not going to hurt you." The attractive stranger pulled their leather jacket tightly around them and ran a hand through their long, brown hair, tossing it back over their shoulder. "We should get out of here. He won't be unconscious for long."

Dazed and confused, Edgar stood like a deer in the headlights, staring at the stranger. They stared back, cocking their head slightly. "Are you coming or not? I understand you're in shock, but it's not safe here." They closed the distance between them before reaching out and taking Edgar's hand like a child. Their hand was warm and soft. Edgar let himself be led to an old car, one of the gasoline-powered models that were being phased out in favor of electric vehicles. He climbed into the passenger seat as the stranger hopped behind the wheel. He sat in silence, trying to process his thoughts and feelings on his crazy morning until they were well away from the scene.

"You must have questions," Edgar's savior said. "I assume you're also in shock. Since it's not safe to hang around, I'm taking you back to my apartment for now. We'll talk whenever you're ready."

"Who are you?" Edgar asked. "Why did you help me?"

"My name is Reis Asher. A friend tipped me off about the Killing Game and I couldn't sit idly by while someone was hunted for sport."

Edgar nodded. "Excuse me for asking, but how should I address you?"

Reis smiled. "Thanks for asking. I prefer they/them pronouns. I'm nonbinary. I assume since you asked, you're relatively familiar with the concept of genders outside the binary?"

"Yeah, absolutely," Edgar smiled warmly. "I have two fathers and I'm bisexual myself. A good number of gender-variant people have passed through my social circle. Oh, and thanks. You know. For saving my life." Edgar stared out of the window, watching as the steel and glass towers of Downtown Anver gave way to the pockmarked concrete constructs of the civil war era that littered Outtown. He was used to seeing the landscape every day, but after what had just happened, he looked at the skyline like he'd never seen it before. The sun was rising, both majestic and frightening, the red horizon seeming like a warning of things to come.

"It seemed like the right thing to do," Reis said. "You were familiar with your attacker?"

"Yeah. Chris was the building maintenance mechanic. He's had a crush on me for years. I never imagined he could ever turn on me..." He closed his eyes, trying to reconcile the Chris he'd known with the desperate man who'd tried to kill him and failing. "He was doing it for his daughter. She needed the million dollars for medical treatment. Reis, what the hell is this Killing Game thing? Maybe you can shed some light."

"I only found out about it this afternoon. I don't know if it's a criminal organization or a group of online trolls looking to play games with people's lives. Either way, it's sick to incite people to kill for money."

"Did they mention a motive? Is there some reason I'm on their hit list?"

"None I know of. It's almost like they want the killings to be random acts of chaos. They used a gumball machine to pick their victim. It's messed up." Reis pulled the car up to the curbside and climbed out. They opened the back door and pulled out a long, black gun case. Edgar opened his door and stepped out. He followed Reis closely as they headed into the decrepit apartment building. A rusty signboard and broken awning suggested the building had once been a hospital, and the stark, worn tile of the corridors seemed to confirm his assumption. Much like his apartment building, only much older and less well-maintained. Reis stepped into the elevator and Edgar followed, glad to have a moment's respite.

"I took a long route to get here," Reis said. "I'm pretty sure we weren't followed, but I circled the block a few times when I wasn't certain."

Edgar nodded. "You seem like you know what you're doing. Military background?"

Reis shook their head. "Nothing beyond mandatory conscription, and I'm sure you served in that regard as well. I happened to grow up in Anver during the civil war."

"Oh." Edger bit back the urge to say, "I'm sorry," knowing such a sentiment was inappropriate and insensitive. "I grew up in Kasyova, so Unification was the first time I ever really interacted with Anver. I love this city though. It's a lot different from Kasyova, and unlike my fathers, I think Anver suits me better."

The elevator screeched a little as it came to a halt and the doors creaked open. Reis led him along a long, dimly lit corridor and swiped a keycard, opening a door at the end of the hallway. The apartment was number 219, but the nine had fallen off and now hung upside down like a six. Reis closed the door behind them and latched and bolted it before letting out a breath they'd clearly been holding.

The apartment seemed slightly cozier than the corridor, though it was no bastion of wealth by a long shot. A tattered couch was covered in a variety of colorful, hand-crocheted blankets, while other mismatched, hand-me-down furniture helped fill the empty spaces in the room. A digital picture frame on the wall cycled through images of people he assumed were Reis's parents, while a flat-panel television took up the majority of one wall.

Reis disappeared into a back room and emerged without the gun case. "Take your shoes off and relax. You're going to be here a while, so you might as well feel at home. Would you like something to eat or drink?"

Edgar slipped out of his sneakers. "I'm not hungry. Not after what I've seen today. I'm struggling to wrap my head around it."

"I can imagine. I have herbal tea if you need something to relax you. Green tea, oolong..." They shrugged. "I take it you're not into tea. You have no idea what I'm talking about, do you?"

"I'm more of a coffee person, myself," Edgar admitted. "Sorry. Feel free to make whatever you think would be best though. I'm open to trying something new— seems to be a day for that. I've never had someone try to murder me before."

"Sadly, you might have to get used to it." Reis busied themself making tea in the tiny kitchenette. Edgar watched Reis's intricate motions as they measured out the leaves, finding the preparation soothing to observe. It was better than thinking about the alternative, at any rate— someone wanted him dead and had set the whole world after him to get it done. It was easier to live in the moment and admire Reis's slender fingers as they lingered on the canister of tea leaves. Their long, chestnut hair as they let it down from its hair tie and it tumbled around their shoulders. Their slender frame as they shed their leather jacket like a second skin and folded it over the back of a chair.

"Here." At the sound of Reis's voice, Edgar woke from his daydream in time to take the teacup from their hands. "We should be safe until dawn. I'm going to call a friend and find out if he called the cops like I asked him to. I want to know why they never came to usher you into protection. I don't like where my mind is going on that— it's possible the cops might be in on the whole thing. It would explain how the Killing Committee is able to offer immunity to the perpetrator. This Killing Game could shed light on corruption at the highest level." Reis looked down at their feet, their eyes cast in shadow. "All the suffering we went through during the war... We thought Unification was our salvation. What if that wasn't really true? What if the Twin City-States have become riddled with corruption?"

"You shouldn't jump to conclusions," Edgar said, sniffing the tea. The aroma was pleasant and soothing. "We don't know anything yet. It's important not to take the Killing Committee's claims at face value. It's far more likely reneging on their promises and watching the killer go down for their crimes—never seeing the money they killed for—is part of their game." Edgar took a sip of the tea, liking the way the warmth spread through his body. The taste wasn't half bad, either, though it could use a little more sugar. "I could get used to this tea. Perhaps today wasn't so bad after all."

Reis managed a cynical snort. "I don't think the seriousness of this has sunk in, yet. I suppose that's understandable. It's a lot to consider." They wandered into the other room and emerged holding a laptop computer. They set it up on Edgar's knees and leaned over him to browse to a webpage. Edgar sat back as the video played, not knowing what to expect. The production values chilled him to the bone. This was no bunch of kids playing trickster. This was a professional operation, backed by a reasonable amount of money and influence. He finished the video and clicked through to another.

"Don't click that, it's—" Reis closed their eyes as one of the murder videos played. Edgar wanted to look away, but sat frozen, unable to tear his gaze away from the horror in front of his eyes. His hands started to tremble, and he could feel the tea ready to come back as bile, burning his throat on the way up.

Reis slammed the laptop shut, halting the audio and video at once. "Stop. This isn't doing you any good."

"They'll kill you too," Edgar whispered. "People like this won't stop at anything to get what they want. There's no need for you to get involved. You can still escape from this. Just take me to Kasyova and I'll disappear. My fathers had friends in the entertainment business who can hide me—smuggle me out of the country."

"This Killing Game isn't limited to the Twin City-States, Edgar. This video is available worldwide. There is nothing that stipulates the killer has to reside here. They could hunt you down wherever you go."

"Then why? Why would you help me, knowing I have no chance of survival?" Edgar stood up, his suspicion and fear growing. "Are you playing the long game, trying to gain my trust before killing me in my sleep? How do I know you're not behind all this? How did you know to swoop in and save me when you did? How is it you say you have no military experience beyond conscription, yet you carry a rifle in that weapons case?"

"My father was an Anver loyalist during the war. He fought the rebels. It's his gun." Reis slumped down on a stool. "I never wanted to use it, but I didn't know what I might need. I saw your face on that broadcast and I had to, Edgar. I *needed* to save you. I don't even know why. Maybe it's because I've spent my whole life thinking I needed to do something worthwhile and I'm twenty-five with absolutely nothing to show for it. Maybe it's because I feel like I'm rotting from the inside out, always unsettled, living with an itch I can't scratch and absolutely no idea what my role is in this world. For once... I felt like I could do something right. Something good. Something that might make a difference. So, I did it."

"I'm not sure I can do this. I'm not a strong person," Edgar admitted. "I was ready to give up, back there. I had accepted my death—thought maybe it was a good thing, if Chris could get the money to save his daughter." Edgar shrugged. "I don't have a lot going for me either, Reis. I quit my job at a big-shot company to be a freelance programmer. I'm fucked because even if I was to go back to my apartment tonight and carry on working, there's no way I could make enough money to cover rent."

"It doesn't matter. That life is over now. For both of us."

"Why would you sacrifice yourself for me?"

"Because I have nothing to lose!" Reis snapped. "There, I said it. I saved your life because I have nothing to live for. Because I'm dying a slow death of despair and maybe, just maybe, if I can save someone else's life, my own will have had some meaning, some purpose."

"That's a fucked-up way to live. What about what you want? Don't you want a partner? Kids, perhaps? What about your parents?"

"My mother died in the war. Dad... He's dead, only his body doesn't know it yet. He mixes his gravy in with his dessert and rambles to the nurses about the war like he was still there. As for a partner... I've never found anyone I really clicked with. I'm not willing to settle for the sake of building a 'family,' I need love—or at least the hope I might one day fall in love—to go on."

"Makes sense." Reis's words struck a chord and Edgar was left wishing he hadn't said a thing. "I'm sorry. I shouldn't have accused you of having an ulterior motive. That wasn't fair."

"It doesn't matter." Reis sighed. "We're both tired and strung out at this point. Let's get some sleep. You can have the couch—it's more comfortable than my bed anyway. We'll reconvene in the morning and see if we can come up with a plan."

Edgar nodded. "Okay. Thanks." He pulled one of the blankets down and covered himself. He fell into a deep sleep before he could consider the fact he hadn't changed out of his jeans.

Chapter Four

REIS

Reis grumbled as they rolled over in their bed, sunlight streaming in through the tattered curtains they'd forgotten to close. They pushed aside the comforter and headed into the bathroom to pee. Their chest ached from wearing their binder for too many hours the previous day, and then they remembered why they'd forgotten to change and sighed.

Edgar. Edgar was in their living room and Reis had absolutely no idea what they were going to do to protect him.

Reis pulled up their pajama pants and headed into the living room, where Edgar was still sound asleep on the couch. One arm was hanging off the sofa onto the floor and his long hair covered his handsome face. He was hot, and cute—but also vulnerable. Reis had thought about asking him to leave in the morning before they'd fallen asleep last night but looking at Edgar now made all those thoughts fly right out of the window.

They couldn't leave Edgar to die in the wilderness of a world out to murder him. Reis imagined themself stalking the murder website, the absence of a video being the only evidence Edgar was still alive. They would wonder what happened to him until the fateful day when his murder video was posted. Reis would watch it, and the last shards of light inside their soul would die.

Reis couldn't let that happen.

Edgar stirred. Reis thought about fleeing into their bedroom—they were never a fan of letting anyone see them sans binder—but if Edgar was going to live here, they couldn't plan on binding twenty-four-seven. They only hoped Edgar wouldn't feel the need to point out the parts of them that tended to cause the most dysphoria. So far, he'd proven himself to be an understanding kind of guy, but even in this mostly post-transphobia world, people had the tendency to slip now and then, causing a bad day where none was intended. Reis hated the wall around themself they tended to build, especially since it had been proven time and time again to be completely unnecessary.

Perhaps they should try tearing that wall down in front of Edgar and see how it all went. Neither of them seemed to have a whole lot to lose—Edgar was a marked man, and Reis was dying inside from loneliness and lack of purpose. If Edgar decided to make Reis's life uncomfortable—well, there was always the door, and then he wouldn't be Reis's responsibility anymore.

"Huh?" Edgar stirred, nearly falling off the couch. "Where am I?" He rubbed his eyes as Reis watched, their arms folded across their chest. Edgar seemed to notice Reis, and Reis nodded.

"Time to get up. You need to shower, and I need to look through my clothes to see if I have anything that might remotely fit you." Reis was pretty sure Ash had left a few things behind when he'd hastily moved out, taking five hundred of Reis's City-State dollars with him, and the two were around the same size. Reis was cautiously optimistic they could find something for Edgar. Though they'd have to change Edgar's appearance. A huge shame, given Edgar's long hair was gorgeous and suited him well, but he stood out like a sore thumb when fashion still favored short hair.

"Thanks. I do appreciate this, and I'm sorry for being a nuisance." Edgar wandered past Reis, and they wondered if Edgar even noticed he was sporting rather obvious morning wood. Reis stifled a giggle and threw him a clean towel.

"You're not a nuisance, but you will be if you don't clean up. You'll lead the killers here with your stench."

If the world had been different and Edgar wasn't being targeted for murder, Reis could see trying to pick him up. They pushed the thought aside and headed to the closet, where Ash's remaining things had been crumpled into a ball and thrown into the back. They still had to call Ash, but they'd been putting it off. Somewhere in the back of Reis's mind they knew Ash could use a million dollars to pay off his gambling debts.

Reis ironed the crumpled clothes and laid them out on the bed for Edgar to decide on what he liked best. They stared down at the carpet as Edgar wandered in, dripping wet, with only a towel for coverage. A blush rose to Reis's cheeks as they slowly lifted their head to meet his gaze.

"Um... You can choose whatever you want to wear. Leave the rest there." Reis brushed past him and headed into the bathroom. They closed the door before soaping up in the shower. Edgar's masculine scent filled the room and Reis felt the kind of stirring they hadn't experienced in a long time. It had been too long since their failed relationship with Ash, and that hadn't been good for a long time before they broke up. Ash's gambling addiction had lived with them like a third partner, one that slowly eroded Reis's trust as objects and money started disappearing. No amount of sex had been worth enduring that—and physical attraction aside, there had never been a spark of anything more. They had been friends with benefits who had almost destroyed their friendship by trying to pretend at love.

Reis sighed. Sleeping with their charge—even if Edgar was interested—was only going to land them both in a world of hurt. If Reis truly wanted to protect Edgar, getting invested either physically or emotionally was probably the worst thing they could do.

That didn't stop the fantasies from popping into Reis's head—Edgar charging into the bathroom, pressing Reis up against the shower wall. He'd kiss their neck, slowly pressing his morning wood inside them as they gave their assent... Yes, yes, yes... Reis moved a finger down between their legs and stroked themself to completion.

After the orgasm came a rush of guilt. Edgar was Reis's houseguest. He was vulnerable. He was in a dangerous and delicate situation. Having such thoughts was plainly inappropriate and a breach of trust. Reis finished showering and stepped out of the water. As they toweled themself down, they thought about omitting their binder to give their ribs a rest, but it felt like armor against the world. They needed it right now, so they wiggled into it, along with a black T-shirt and a pair of jeans they'd brought into the bathroom with them.

Reis emerged from the bathroom, thinking about breakfast, when the pop of a gunshot followed by breaking glass sounded through the apartment. Reis's instinct was to drop to the ground and crawl across the carpet. "Edgar!" They crawled to Edgar's prone body in the living room.

"I'm okay," Edgar whispered. Another gunshot whizzed over their heads and buried itself in the digital picture frame over the mantel.

"They know you're here," Reis whispered. "We need to go." They were glad Edgar was fully dressed and the only thing he'd missed out on was breakfast. "In the hallway there's a storage closet. Get inside and shut the door. I have to get my rifle. I'll meet you there." They parted without another word. Reis crawled across the room, dragged their leather jacket down from the chair, and pulled it on. They raised themself to a crouch and shuffled into the back room where they quickly stuffed their handgun and knife into their belt before grabbing the rifle case.

In the living room, they opened the case, pulled out the rifle, and loaded a magazine. Reis wasn't sure if they'd be able to shoot but looking down the scope would give them an idea of how many people they were facing. They stood next to the window and pushed the rifle's muzzle out through the frame, scanning the buildings opposite for a sniper. Seeing nothing, they moved their gaze to the ground, where a couple of figures were hunkered down behind vehicles on the street. One peeked their head out. They were clad in black and it was hard to get a look at their face. Reis moved the scope until a figure was in their crosshairs. Fine. Their anonymity would make this easier.

The figure looked right up at the scope with familiar green eyes, and Reis's finger paused on the trigger as they recognized Ash. *Damn it. I was right. This whole thing was a play.* A high-stakes poker game for a million dollars in cryptocurrency. It had been easy for Ash to call Reis, to appeal to their sense of justice by seeming horrified. Of course, Ash had known Reis would be enough of a sucker to save Edgar and bring him here. He'd set the stage for the perfect ambush.

Reis pulled back from their position at the window and stowed the rifle back in its case. They weren't going to shoot Ash, even though he deserved it. Reis swallowed their anger like a bitter pill. Emotions were only going to get in the way right now. They needed to get to Edgar and get out of here. The longer they let themself be pinned down, the higher the chance a strike team of Ash's hired thugs would use their advantage to storm the building. Reis swallowed as they headed out into the hallway just in time to see a Molotov sail in through an open window. The flames caught on a curtain. Whoever had thrown it must have known the old wooden building would go up like a tinderbox and flush them out. Reis opened the closet door and gestured for Edgar to come out. Edgar saw the burning hallway and his eyes widened. Reis shook their head, urging him to let it go.

It was only stuff. No, that wasn't true. It was all Reis had to show for their life, and it was going up in smoke. Their piano—that instrument of such beautiful, soothing music—would be nothing more than ashes in an hour. Worse, it was likely to be the first of many sacrifices Reis would have to make to keep Edgar alive. Reis hit the fire alarm and yelled, causing multiple residents to open their doors. Children started crying as their parents barked at them in alarmed tones. Reis grabbed Edgar's hand and led him down the back stairwell amidst all the commotion and chaos. They were pressed so close together in the mass of bodies, no sniper could get a clear shot as they spilled out onto the street. They were able to slip down an alley to where Reis's car was parked.

"My car—in the lot—it was rigged to blow," Edgar hissed in warning.

"What else do you propose? We're sitting ducks if we go on foot. We have to take the risk." Reis jumped into the driver's seat and started the vehicle before Edgar could protest further. They breathed a sigh of relief when the engine turned over and the car didn't explode. Seemingly satisfied, Edgar climbed in beside them. Reis hit the accelerator, speeding away from the scene.

"Where now?" Edgar asked. "If they found us at your apartment, where else could we go to be safe?"

"I don't know," Reis admitted. "Let me think." They let out a long sigh. "It was all a setup. Ash—a former boyfriend of mine—he was the one who told me about the Killing Game. He knew I'd try to save you, that I'd be dumb enough to bring you back to my apartment. I can't believe I let him use me."

"I'm sorry about your apartment." Edgar bowed his head.

"I'm sorry too," Reis said. "That piano was my last birthday present from my mother before she died. I can never get it back."

"You should let me out. You've given up too much already trying to save me. You don't owe me—or anyone—anything."

"They know I'm a part of this now. I chose to paint a target on my head, so I can't complain I was targeted. I knew the risks going into this. I'm not going to give up now it's started to hurt."

"Reis..."

"Human life is more valuable than objects, even ones with sentimental value. This world has forgotten the value of people. Drowning in our own despair, we can't see the most important things are right in front of us. Maybe that's why the Killing Game exists, Edgar. Maybe it's some twisted goon's idea of a sacrifice to restore the value of life by showing how much it hurts when it's taken away from us."

"Restoring the value of life by destroying it? That's some pretzel-shaped logic right there."

"I didn't say the Killing Committee was right. Obviously, I don't agree with murder, or I wouldn't be here. If it was so easy for me to pull the trigger, I'd have killed Ash with my rifle and not thought twice about it. But I hesitated. I couldn't do it. I might not have been in love with him, but I cared for him, once upon a time."

"I'm sorry," Edgar repeated.

"You need to stop apologizing," Reis said. "You of all people didn't choose your fate. You never wanted to be a part of this. So, stop complaining I'm trying to save your life. Stop insinuating you're a pain in the ass and the world would be better off without you."

"I've caused you a lot of pain and misery thus far," Edgar pointed out. "So, I'd say I have a lot to be sorry for. Besides, I can't shake the feeling there has to be a reason for all this. I don't believe events are truly random. I was on that list of names to be pulled for a reason. I've done something or wronged someone enough they want me dead. Worse is I don't know why—which means I'm probably such an insensitive bastard I've hurt someone without even realizing it."

"Did you have any acrimonious breakups? Or maybe someone was in love with you and felt like you shunned them?" Reis shrugged when Edgar shook his head. "Do we really need a motive? Does it make it better if some stalker put you on a list because they couldn't get over you, or because you stole their lunch money in kindergarten?"

Edgar smiled. "I never stole anyone's lunch money, but wow, that'd be quite the escalation."

"I figured—you seem way too sensitive for that. I suspect you were the one who had your lunch money stolen."

"Yeah, pretty much. I'm your average nerd—only people like to tell me I'm pretty hot. It seems to draw the kind of attention I'd rather not have, really—people who don't like me once they find out my primary interest is writing instructions for computers to follow." Edgar leaned back in the passenger seat. "I used to have a lot of friends in college, but they tapered off once they realized I wasn't interested in maintaining false friendships. I want to be around people who like me for who I really am, not based on my looks."

"I don't suppose those computer talents come with any hacking skills? It sure would be helpful if we could get a handle on who the Killing Committee is," Reis observed.

Edgar sighed. "I'm sure they've covered their tracks far better than my amateur digging could uncover. These folks are pros—they're not going to leave their home address in a public domain registry. Besides, the only computer we had access to just went up in smoke."

"Yeah. Any ideas on our next move?"

"We need to rent a room. Cash only. No questions asked. Maybe this thing will blow over if we give it enough time."

Reis shook their head. "A motel room? That's way too obvious. Any bounty hunter worth their salt will be looking in those places."

"Not a motel room. A room above a store, or an office—somewhere where nobody will even think to look for me. We need to hide in plain sight."

Reis chewed on a hangnail. "I may have an idea. My mother used to own a store. She passed it on to me in her will, but there's not much left. I shuttered the business and left the building to the elements, but it still technically belongs to me."

"That's not going to work. They'll be combing through everything that belongs to you. They'll leave no stone unturned."

"I said it only 'technically' belongs to me. It was bequeathed to my deadname. I never bothered to change the title on the building when I changed my name."

"They could still trace it. Court records and all," Edgar pointed out.

"Eventually. It would take time, and time is what we need right now. Time to plan our next move. Unless you have any better ideas?"

"Okay. Let's go," Edgar said.

Reis turned the corner, plotting out a route to a place they'd once called home and wondering how many ghosts would be waiting to greet them there.

Chapter Five

EDGAR

Edgar felt a sense of trepidation as they passed through Outtown to some of the neighborhoods that had been completely abandoned after the war. Few people ever came to the Forgotten Streets of Anver, though the radiation from the suitcase dirty bomb the rebels had detonated had degraded enough to make living in the district mostly safe.

Edgar sat quietly as Reis pulled the car off the street into a small jetty. In a normal place, they would have been blocking traffic, but here it camouflaged the car well enough to avoid unwanted attention. Edgar got out of the car and helped Reis pull an old tarp over the back end of the car, hiding the clean, current license plate and enabling the vehicle to blend in with its surroundings.

Edgar followed Reis to the front of the building. The windows had been broken and boarded up, but the door was still intact. Reis unlocked it with a rusty set of keys and stepped inside, setting off a bell which made the pair of them jump. The door slammed shut behind them, but the glass window let in enough light to allow them to see the dusty countertop and the faded silk flowers still sitting on shelves.

"Your mother was a florist?" Edgar asked.

"Yeah. I used to help her when I was a kid. I hated it. She said flowers made people happy, but I always thought the opposite. People always came for funerals, especially during the war, or for lovers they'd wronged. That and making bouquets always seemed to set my dysphoria off like crazy." They walked through the shelves, looking through old displays and blowing the dust off a glass case full of trophies. "I didn't know who I was back then. I knew I hated being called a girl, and the flowers tended to reinforce everyone's assumption I was a girl." They reached down and picked up a silk rose. "Now, I can appreciate they're pretty. I wish I'd been able to do that when Mom was alive, but I was so busy rejecting everything to do with femininity. I wasn't ready to accept there are male and female aspects to my soul, and the existence of one doesn't cancel the other out." Reis shrugged. "I'm sorry. Here I am, going on about myself. I doubt you want to hear me ramble on about gender."

"On the contrary, I find it interesting. It sure beats thinking about when we're going to get attacked again."

"We need to come up with some kind of concrete plan. We can't keep running. There's nowhere else to go. We need to make sure we're such a pain they give up the fight."

"It won't matter." Edgar paced the room. "I've been thinking—how do we get out of this, Reis? Short of taking down the Killing Committee, they're never going to stop coming after me. I could change my name, my appearance—everything about myself—and they'd still find me eventually."

"The alternative is giving up," Reis replied. "Are you willing to walk outside with your hands in the air and get gunned down in cold blood so someone else can collect a cash reward?"

Edgar shrugged. "I don't see a reasonable alternative."

"It's too early to give up. We've barely started. I can't imagine Ash contacted the police, so I'm planning to get on that today. They may be able to offer you entry into a witness protection program. Once the incentive for killing you is gone, you'll be able to start over."

"Start over and do what? I'm not sure I'll ever be able to trust anyone again. I'll have to move back to Kasyova and change my name. Even then, I'll be looking behind me every time I walk down the street. What kind of a life is that?"

"The life I lead," Reis said. "The things I saw in the civil war will haunt me for the rest of my life. Even after years of therapy, I'll never be able to go out without a weapon on me, just in case."

"I'm sorry. I didn't know it was that bad." Edgar sat down on a rickety old chair behind the counter and drew lines in the dust. "You have a tendency to make me feel guilty, you know that? You've lived this terrible life of yours with far more grace than I have my spoiled, loving one. I haven't had to struggle with my identity—I seemed to fall into being bi, and nobody ever batted an eyelid. Kasyova was always at peace, even before Unification. Until yesterday, I had no idea what it means to live in fear for your life. My kind, loving dads died of old age because they had me rather late in life, but it was a peaceful thing for both of them, and I never felt like they wanted for anything at their end. Kinda makes me feel like a waste, you know? I want for a lot of things, but I'm too lazy to go for them. Even now, I feel like it's easier to give up than really fight for my life. Like, it would be more convenient for everyone if I go into the back and hang myself. It's not like I want to die... But the idea of putting your life at risk just to save this life which has so far been rather devoid of purpose seems ridiculous."

"I don't know why, but your blasé attitude to life makes me even angrier than the Killing Commission's." Reis slammed their hand down on the counter. "I'm going into the back to call the cops and then I'm going to scope out the neighborhood. If you want to drown in your own tears, be my guest—but right now, I don't want to hear about it." Reis stormed off into the back, leaving Edgar to let out a long sigh. He'd long since quit smoking, but he was starting to get a craving like an itch he couldn't scratch. Reis seemed to get under his skin in ways he hadn't anticipated. Why the hell were they so desperate to save him? Why couldn't they give up and leave him to get shot? He sat and thought about what it might feel like to actually die and chewed his lip. No, he didn't want to die. Not really. It was easier to talk about it like it was some distant possibility happening to someone else, like it didn't really matter and would be instant and painless.

He hadn't had the chance to process anything that had happened to him thus far and so he sat and ran his mind over it, from the crazy events of the day before in the apartment block up to right now. It was obvious in hindsight Chris had planned to burn him with the hot water in order to have him call for maintenance. He'd been lured to the basement, where Chris had tried to choke him out with the rope. Thinking back to that moment caused an uncomfortable tightness in his windpipe, and he touched his throat now to feel a line of nasty bruises and welts across his neck.

He wanted to go to Reis, to say he was sorry, to thank them again for putting their own neck on the line to save his worthless ass, but he could hear Reis on the phone talking about the desperate nature of their situation. He closed his eyes to listen in. What a person Reis was, going through all this shit for him. To save him. All he'd given Reis in return was a total lack of fucks about the life Reis had saved.

He didn't deserve a guardian angel but somehow, he'd gotten one.

The back room fell quiet, and Reis emerged. Edgar opened his mouth to say something but couldn't summon anything beyond the pathetic sounding "I'm sorry." He remained silent as Reis walked by him without a word, sniper rifle slung over their back. They opened the shop door, the bell tinkling, and disappeared into the morning fog.

Edgar busied himself cleaning, trying to keep his mind off things. Every creak the old building made caused him to jump, and he grew more anxious as the hours passed. It was nightfall before Reis returned. They locked the door behind them and headed into the back room. Edgar followed, desperate for news.

"There's not a lot to report. As I expected, the police seem to think the Killing Game is nothing more than a prank, the murder videos fabricated—but they are looking into it. I don't expect a lot from them, though, which means we're on our own." Reis unloaded a backpack from their shoulders and placed it down on a dusty counter. "I got us food and blankets. I had to stash my rifle for a while, but fortunately it was still there when I returned."

"I've been doing some thinking," Edgar said. "If we can't count on the police, maybe we should skip town. Get the hell out of here while we still can. You can take me as far as the border, and then I can take it from there. I can get off the grid entirely. Find a cabin in rural Yuvego, do some work under the table, throw away this identity, and start a new life."

"Would you be happy, making your living as a day laborer in some foreign, rural small town?" Reis asked.

"I'd be alive. Once they realized you had no idea where I was, you'd be safe too. They can't kill you—that's against the rules. They don't get immunity for it. The Killing Game would move along, easier targets would come up. It's not impossible to disappear."

"No, I suppose not." Reis almost seemed disappointed, and Edgar realized he was taking away Reis's sense of purpose.

"You'd be safe, Reis. Your mission would be complete. You've done more for me than I ever could have asked for. I'm grateful—more than you'll ever know."

"I don't think I can go back to the life I had before knowing the Killing Committee is out there, choosing more targets for their sick game. It's not that simple, Edgar. I've seen what humanity is capable of and I can't just lock it up in a box and ignore it."

"Do you really expect to bring down a consortium of individuals so rich and powerful they're willing to give away a million dollars to shake things up for their entertainment? A group with so much influence they're above the law itself? Get real."

"I have to try," Reis said. "When Unification happened, I didn't celebrate along with everyone else. It wasn't that I wasn't happy to see an end to the war and strife that followed; I was happier than anyone. But it all seemed so pointless. Why did all those people die in the war when the answer lay in our neighbor peacefully assimilating us all along? What was it all for? Those deaths were senseless—just like the Killing Game. There's no point or purpose to war except chaos. My mother died for *nothing*, Edgar. Absolutely nothing."

"But she didn't live for nothing. She made people happy with her flowers. You can see it in this place. Look around you."

"What are you saying?"

"Maybe you have a calling—but that calling isn't throwing your life away to save mine. You say you want to preserve order and to make a difference in the world. Have you ever considered becoming a police officer?"

Reis laughed. "Many times." They sat down against the wall and drew lines in the dirt on the floorboards. "I never seemed to gather enough courage to apply to the academy. That's my life in a nutshell. I'm never brave enough to commit to anything."

"You committed yourself to saving me." Edgar sat down next to Reis. Even from this distance, it was possible to feel their body heat radiating outward, and Edgar had to fight the urge to move closer in the cold evening. He pulled one of the blankets from the paper bag instead and spread it over his legs.

They shared a small meal of fresh fruit and crackers, their sole light a candle Reis had purchased. Edgar watched the flame flicker, a single, wavering beacon of light in a world of darkness. His life was as fragile as that tiny flame, apt to be blown out in the strong wind of the Killing Committee's demands to have him killed.

"Do you have any regrets?" Reis asked. They, too, were bundled up beneath a blanket, staring at the flame. Edgar wondered if they were having the same grim thoughts he was, the realization they were living on borrowed time.

"Not regrets, per se," Edgar replied. "More...things I wish I'd made time for—people, primarily. I wish I'd made more time for people."

"That surprises me," Reis arched an eyebrow. "You seem like someone who should be surrounded by others. You're intelligent, charming, and personable. You don't push people away like I do."

"I've done nothing except try to push you away. 'Reis, you should leave me at the border. Reis, you should stop protecting me.' I don't know what it is, but I'm afraid to rely on others. It feels too much like failure. The idea my life is in someone else's hands and I'm completely helpless to do anything about it is too much."

"You're not helpless. You had the same military training I did. I have a spare gun." Reis leaned over into their gun case and took out a pistol. They handed it to Edgar, who took it and looked at it like it was an alien artifact. "If you want me to leave you alone, then prove you can defend yourself. Otherwise, you're prey for the Killing Game. I won't accept that. It's not only about you but this whole damn situation. Something like the Killing Game can't be allowed to exist."

The candle blew out, a sudden draft plunging them into darkness. Edgar was acutely aware someone was watching them and had been the entire time—and Reis had realized far sooner than he had.

"How many?" Edgar whispered. Reis held up four fingers and reached for their sniper rifle. Edgar took a deep breath, trying to still his hammering heart, certain it was giving him away to their attackers. Reis stood back-to-back with him, and Edgar realized there was nobody else he'd rather have cover him. As strange as they could be for being the ultimate Good Samaritan, Edgar respected them for it. So long as there were people like Reis in the world to counter evils like the Killing Game, the human race would be all right.

The gunshots rang out so suddenly that Edgar nearly jumped out of his skin. The front room of the shop was being swept with automatic weapons fire. Whoever these guys were, they acted with the absolute certainty their prey was here in this building, and they were professionals with money and bullets to spare.

It was unlikely they'd get out of this alive.

Edgar turned and whispered into Reis's ear, his lips so close and his voice quiet like a lover's whisper. "You don't have to die here. You can go. Leave me."

Reis only smiled. They brushed Edgar's hair away from his ear and leaned in close. "I think it's about time I committed to something, don't you?" They pulled away. Edgar could smell a faint hint of cigarettes and coffee on their breath and wondered if they'd spent the day at some coffee shop, looking out at the gray Anver sky, to come to this conclusion.

Reis was so close Edgar thought for the briefest moment they might kiss, and he wasn't averse to the prospect. Something stirred inside him—an eagerness to protect Reis, who had put so much on the line for him for no other reason than because it was the right thing to do.

A bullet hit the plaster at the far end of the room, and Edgar gripped his pistol tightly. The moment had slipped away, and he was left with a thousand things he wanted to say now they were out of time. The window at the end of the room that led to the greenhouse shattered, and a black-suited figure rappelled in. The door at the other end of the room burst open, revealing three similarly suited figures, all heavily armed.

They'd come to kill Edgar, and this time, there was no doubt they'd succeed.

Chapter Six

REIS

Reis inhaled deeply. Time seemed to slow as they raised the rifle. They'd never killed anyone. The conscripted forces did little in times of peace. The million weapons drills they'd performed didn't prepare them for the moment when life met death and only death could prevail. They couldn't believe how oddly calm they were in the face of it all, as they raised the rifle and took a shot at the figure standing by the window. The shot rang out so much louder than Reis had expected, the kickback threatening to break their nose. The figure crumpled to the ground.

Next to them, Edgar hesitated. Reis could feel the tightness in his muscles, the guarded nature of his stance. He couldn't shoot. Something in Edgar refused, a mental barrier Reis knew he'd never be able to push through, even with his life on the line. Some people weren't born to be killers, and apparently Edgar was one of these people. Reis raised their rifle and shot the figures, watching them slump to the ground like faceless shadows. They didn't even stop to admire their handiwork before grabbing Edgar's hand and jumping through the open window into the greenhouse.

"More?" Edgar asked. Reis nodded with an affirmative grunt, fearing words would break their concentration. They couldn't afford to think, only plan and execute. Thinking would bring with it the inevitable force of conscience, the horror of knowing Reis had taken four lives this night. Four people who would never go home to the ones who loved them. It was hard to blame them when something like the Killing Game existed like a carrot, luring the desperate and vulnerable into bad decisions.

Reis scanned the greenhouse and took a shot at a figure rappelling in from the roof. Another one panicked, lost their footing, and crashed through the brittle glass to land like a sack of potatoes at Reis's feet.

They were so focused on the threat from above they didn't even see the threat from behind until they heard a shot ring out. They turned to see Edgar drop their gun and crumple to the ground. Reis saw another aggressor lower themself from the roof, and took a shot without thinking, reloading while trying to glance at Edgar. There was a dead man in the doorway. If Edgar had been shot, then he'd also shot one of their attackers.

The assault seemed to stop. The rotors of a helicopter floated up and away, and Reis realized the would-be assassins been using it to attack them from the roof of the building. Scanning for more threats, Reis decided the coast was clear and dropped their rifle. They rushed to Edgar's side. To their horror, Edgar was holding his hands over a wound in his stomach, trying to keep in the blood that seeped through his fingers like water escaping a broken glass.

"Edgar!" Reis's voice was cracked and dry, their throat tight. Tears sprang to their eyes, surprising themself more than anyone. How long had it been since they'd felt strongly enough about anything to cry?

"You need to go... Reis..." Edgar squeezed his eyes shut, wincing with the pain.

"Don't be stupid!" Reis yelled. "We're going to get you to a hospital."

"Why? So they can put a pillow over my face while I sleep?"

"I'll guard your bedside. I won't let anything happen to you!"

"If I didn't know better, Reis, I'd say you had feelings for me." Edgar smiled; a charming grin that would have made Reis laugh if they hadn't been sobbing. He raised one bloody hand to wipe Reis's tear away. "It's okay. Really, it is."

Reis wasn't sure if he was talking about his feelings or his inevitable death, but they were filled with a sudden rush of desperation so powerful it filled their body with strength.

"This isn't how it ends!" Reis said. They reached for their cellphone. "My friend's been shot. I need help. The address is..."

"Reis, I'll never make it. I've been gut shot. We both served, we know what that means..." Edgar closed his eyes. "I'm lucky to have met someone like you. I think I was waiting for this moment my entire life... To meet someone like you and give them a little push..."

"What are you talking about?" Reis asked.

"Do you...believe in fate?"

"Only in the sense we make our own."

"Then make this. Become a police officer. Find out who's behind the Killing Game and bring them to justice. You can do it. I know you can." Edgar opened his eyes and managed a smile. "I think...that's your fate."

The sound of sirens grew close. Reis stood as the EMTs stepped over the bodies of their assailants in the doorway to render medical assistance. A police SWAT team swarmed in, and Reis raised their hands in surrender. They closed their eyes as Edgar was taken away on a stretcher, holding back the flood of agony that threatened to tear them apart. A police officer bound their wrists in handcuffs and took their sniper rifle as evidence, but Reis didn't care. The color seemed to have left the world, the foliage of the wild plants taking over the greenhouse seeming more brown than green. The florist shop seemed like a strange place instead of the home where they'd spent a good portion of their childhood. They offered no resistance as they were taken outside and bundled into a police car. Red and blue lights lit up the night, but all Reis could think about was Edgar. Even if the gunshot didn't kill him, he was still in danger. Any EMT who knew about the Killing Game could finish him off quietly and obtain video footage without arousing suspicion. People died on the operating table all the time. The Killing Committee hadn't specified one had to make a violent kill to obtain the money. Air in a syringe would do the trick just as well.

Heavy thoughts weighed Reis down as the police car sped through the narrow Anver streets. A torrential downpour began, raindrops landing on the roof of the vehicle like a thousand tiny rocks. Even with the ringing in their ears from the gunfight, the noise was deafening. The officers turned the wipers to full, slowing in the dark water to ensure their safety. It seemed to take forever to reach the police station. The short walk from the car up the station steps soaked Reis and they felt like a drowned rat as they sat in the interrogation room, water dripping from their hair and clothing. They resigned themself to the long wait, knowing there was nothing they could do for Edgar now. Hopefully, no assassin would be waiting among the operating staff, and Edgar would likely be in surgery for hours. If he didn't succumb to his wounds before then... No, Reis wouldn't accept that as a possibility. They'd come this far. Edgar wasn't going to die now.

The interrogation room door opened. Two detectives came in and closed the door behind them. One was short, stocky, and feminine, while the other was a tall, masculine person. Both wore shirts, ties, and pants.

The woman spoke first. "Reis Asher. I'm Agent Emily Vos and this is Agent Gareth Grady."

"Nice to meet you."

Vos didn't return the nicety. "You were hard to trace, Reis. A court sealed your records. That's not a normal procedure during a gender marker and name change anymore. Perhaps you'd like to volunteer that information? Don't get me wrong, I'm not asking you to deadname yourself. We just need to know a few things about you."

"If you're asking me, it's because you already know who I am." Reis bowed their head. "My father is Elias Torell, hero of the civil war and the architect of Unification. That's what you wanted me to confirm, isn't it?"

"If you'd only told us this when you filed your police report, we might have taken this 'Killing Game' a bit more seriously," Agent Grady piped in.

Reis blew out air. This was why they hadn't joined the police force. Reputation was everything in Anver and the Twin City-States at large. Always had been, always would be. As the child of a war hero, doors would always open for Reis when people inevitably realized who their father was. Somehow, they always seemed to find out. Having the court seal their deadname when they'd changed away from it hadn't seemed to help.

"The name of my father doesn't change my actions. I killed those men. It was self-defense, but I killed them. I have no regrets. Edgar would have become another victim of the Killing Game otherwise, and I couldn't let that happen. So, slap me with whatever charges you like. Strip me of my reputation. I don't care."

"If you're locked up in jail, you can't help Edgar." Agent Vos shook her head. "And we very much need you to help him."

"I don't follow," Reis said. "Can't you assign Edgar a protection detail now you're aware the Killing Game is real? Even better, put him in a witness protection program."

Agent Vos pulled a lipstick from her pocket. She twisted the bottom, but nothing came out. Reis saw a green light on the bottom blink, and realized it was no lipstick at all, but some kind of electronic device.

"We don't have a lot of time," Agent Grady pointed out. "We can only jam the video feed for a couple of minutes. Reis, the Killing Game conspiracy goes all the way to the top. We've been investigating it for a year now.

Every time we get close, doors slam shut in our face. Evidence goes missing. Along with the video's claim the perpetrator will walk free, what we've found links people in the police force, the government, and the military with the Killing Game."

"Why?" Reis's eyes widened. "I'd wondered as much... But what point does this serve?"

"Come now, Reis. You of all people should know not everybody was happy when the tanks rolled in and Unification was declared without a single shot against Kasyova. Foreign powers were especially displeased to watch Kasyova grow in power as they assimilated Anver. But it's impossible to overthrow the government when it's so popular. The people love being a part of Kasyova. It's the old guard who want it back. The nationalists and the rebels who never liked Kasyovan ideals and freedoms."

"The best way to get there is to destabilize the government, little by little, eroding the people's happiness and sense of security," Vos elaborated. "What better way to do that then to introduce chaos? The Killing Game isn't their only tool, but it is a powerful one. When they see ordinary citizens being killed, the populace begins to feel helpless. The government and the police want to act, but they are already compromised from within."

"What do you want me to do?" Reis asked. "I'm only one person."

"A person with conviction," Grady said. "You were willing to put your life on the line to save someone you'd never met. You're exactly the kind of person the Twin City-States need right now. What we need you to do is go on doing what you're doing. Protect Edgar Tobias. The longer he stays alive, the more frustrated the Killing

Committee will become. Without handing out a prize, they'll grow desperate. They've never had a target live more than a day, and suddenly they have one who's lived three, slowing their timeline considerably. You must have noticed those men you killed were no ordinary people, but trained soldiers. We believe that was the Committee taking matters into their own hands, but it was careless of them. They showed their hand. We were able to trace back dog tags on the soldiers' bodies to a mercenary group allied with a group of former Anverite rebels, and from there, we traced a payment back to an offshore bank account of a shell corporation. We're pretty sure we know who one of the members of the Killing Committee is, now—Tony Anvas, owner of the Anvas Media Group. He disavowed the rebels after the war, but the picture we're piecing together is that his statement was unequivocally false and he's working behind the scenes to overthrow the Twin City-State government."

"They can change the rules at any time for maximum impact," Reis said. "What's to stop them choosing another target?"

"They're not actually selecting people at random, though to the untrained eye the people they are choosing seem normal enough. They're picking off the children and grandchildren of Kasyovan cultural icons for maximum impact. Edgar Tobias is the son of famous singer-songwriter duo The Soulmates—didn't he tell you?" When Reis shook their head, Grady continued. "Sure, they could choose someone else and try to push aside the fact Edgar slipped through their grasp—and we're sure they'll do so—but their goal is not only to create fear, but to slowly destroy the legacies of those who enrich Kasyovan culture in hopes they'll subtly erase Kasyovan influence and society entirely."

Vos spoke up. "We know the odds are against you, but we're not asking you to do this alone. We'll help as much as we can. We'll keep in contact and provide you with safe houses and weapons. In the meantime, we need Edgar to keep breathing so the Killing Committee keeps making mistakes like the one they made today. We need to push their timeline back as much as possible with the least amount of bloodshed. We need to make them desperate so they expose themselves."

"I'm not a police officer. All I have is the basic training I received in the military. What makes you think I can do this?" Reis stood. "What's to stop these corrupt elements from erasing the evidence, so you can never bring these beasts to trial?"

"You let us worry about that," Grady said. "We have a few safeguards in place. We're tired of watching these murderers get away with it. As for you—you have a level of resolve we rarely see in this modern era. You truly are your father's child."

"And my mother's. She may never have had the reputation you hold so dear, but she was a hell of a woman." Reis tugged against their handcuffs. "I'll do it, but not because of who I am or who Edgar is, or even to protect the government. I'm doing this because it's the right thing to do. Because life is not something to be casually destroyed for the sake of a game of chess."

"We're out of time," Grady explained. "We'll be releasing you without charges. We'll be escorting you to a safe house as soon as Edgar is well enough to leave the hospital. We'll send along further instructions as needed. Good luck, Reis."

"Same to you," Reis said, wondering where the safest place would be to spend the night. Exhaustion tugged at their senses, but their mind was whirling, and they knew they wouldn't be able to sleep even if they did find a bed. To imagine a conspiracy was one thing, but to have actual confirmation the Killing Committee was trying to bring down the government was quite another. Reis wished their father was still lucid, but even if he was, going to see him was a risk they couldn't afford to take. No, their father had taught Reis everything they could about the ways of the world. It was up to Reis to follow through, protect Edgar, and hope it was enough to make the Killing Committee slip up.

Grady unlocked the handcuffs and Reis rubbed their wrists as they took a pen and signed off on a mountain of paperwork. Vos brought in their things and laid them on the table; Reis's sniper rifle, packed away in its black case, the pistol they'd lent Edgar, complete with Edgar's dried blood on the grip, and the various combat knives and the backpack they'd had on their person. Their heart lurched, and Reis felt a sudden need to get to the hospital as soon as possible. If Edgar had died on the table, all Reis's efforts would have been for nothing.

They left the station. The downpour had slowed to a steady rain, and the smells of the wet city streets wafted up to Reis's nose like a comforting old friend. They'd always loved the rain, especially at night, when the billboards and neon lights reflected off the slick roads and sidewalks. Anver's famous Hospital Tower beckoned to them, the circular skyscraper's light rings glowing white to indicate all was quiet as far as admissions. Red meant the hospital was at full capacity, with orange, blue, and finally white for lower levels of activity. It had glowed red often during the war years, with active shelling in and around the city. Nowadays it was often the first indication of a major accident before official word broke.

Reis broke into a steady sprint, knowing every second they took could be the second that allowed an assassin to sneak into Edgar's room.

Double doors yielded to Reis as they reached the base of the tower. The vestibule beckoned them in, a smiling, pink-haired receptionist sitting at a white desk at the center of the circular entryway that formed the base of the tower.

"I'm looking for Edgar Tobias," Reis said. "Multiple gunshot wounds. I'm—I'm his partner." The words felt uncomfortable in their mouth, as if they'd spoken a truth without realizing it until the words were out in the world. Reis had meant it as a lie—the hospital wouldn't allow a mere friend to come visit someone in such critical condition—and yet the word partner made their guts twist into excited, terrified knots.

"Edgar Tobias has no partner on file," the receptionist said. "I'd be lying if I said you're the first person to come looking for him." They gave Reis a glance that instantly told them this pencil-pusher knew about the bounty on Edgar's head and intended, in some way, to attempt collection. Suddenly, the low mood lighting didn't seem so welcoming, the smile on the receptionist's face appearing more like a sneer. Reis fought the urge to show their hand and risk being detained by campus police by making a bolt for the elevator and instead smoothed their expression, meeting the receptionist's faux-blue eyes with their own brown ones in a battle of wills.

The receptionist, either fearing a stronger foe or considering themselves to have the advantage, broke the staring contest with a smile. "Well, *sweetie*," they drawled, "he's still in surgery. You're welcome to go up to the third floor and wait. He's in Operating Room Four."

"Thanks," Reis managed, hurrying to the elevator bank in the back, aware of the receptionist's eyes on them the whole time. They breathed a short sigh of momentary relief when the doors slid closed and the elevator rose upward.

Edgar was alive—but for how long? Reis shook their head, trying to shake some of the rain free. They were aware of their hair forming dank ringlets around their face, and the pull of the binder against their ribs, their chest muscles itching to get out so they could *breathe* properly.

With a chime, the elevator doors swung open. Reis sidestepped a gurney being wheeled into the elevator and made a beeline for the information desk.

"Edgar Tobias," Reis whispered, swearing they noticed a dozen sets of ears perking up from the nearby waiting room.

"He's a popular guy," the chubby, handsome young man behind the counter said with a wide smile. "Must be loved. But then, I always did have a soft spot for The Soulmates. I can't believe anyone would take a gun to the sweet little child they paid tribute to in their hit 'Everything But The Son.' Of course, he's a man now, so who knows what trouble he's gotten himself into, but still..."

Reis looked around at the collection of people gathered in the waiting room. There was a Kasyovan busker with a guitar and dreads, tuning his instrument. An older woman with long gray hair sat drawing in a small sketchbook. A few mixed queer couples of all genders and none sat hugging and holding hands. These weren't killers. These were people from the world of Kasyovan entertainment—a community come together to protect one of their own. Reis felt the terror slip away from them at this heartwarming scene. Reis wasn't alone in wanting to help Edgar. Edgar did have friends—or at least his fathers did. Not that one of these friends couldn't turn on him, but this collection of creators and artists seemed the furthest thing from threatening Reis had ever seen.

They wandered away from the desk with a "thanks" and into the throng of entertainers. They sat the case with their sniper rifle in it down beside a chair and took a seat. The guitarist sat opposite Reis, with their guitar case open for donations. A few Kasyovan dollars lay in the worn velvet lining. Reis felt moved and reached into their pocket, pulled some coins out, and threw them in.

"Hey, thanks!" The busker shifted in their chair, inspired to play. They started the first few chords of a song that sounded vaguely familiar to Reis and began to sing:

> "There's no greater sweetness in life, I thought
> At least that's what I'd been taught
> But they always sat and told us of fun
> About everything but the son."

Reis smiled a little, realizing this was the song the man at the desk had referenced. The song about Edgar, written and performed by two loving parents who were proud of their son. It was enough to bring tears to Reis's eyes, and they wiped them away, suddenly embarrassed. As a fellow musician, they could understand the moving power of music, but to know Edgar was so loved was comforting. The busker smiled, offering one hand to Reis, who stood and shook it firmly.

"I'm Teon Escher, they/them, all love," Teon said. They grinned widely, white teeth standing out against the dark hue of their skin. "I'm sensing a kindred spirit nearby."

"Yeah," Reis said, their last barriers falling. Despite their two countries becoming interlinked, Reis had never really walked in the same circles as the warm, open, Kasyovan queer community, and they regretted it now. Reis suspected if it was them on the table, few would show up and sit vigil for them, let alone sing. Anverite society didn't look down on anyone, but favored those who kept their personal feelings and relationships in the private sphere. That unspoken rule forced most people to take on two personas to live a successful professional life. "You'd be right. I'm Reis Asher, they/them as well."

"What do you play, Reis?" Teon gestured to the black case tucked away between Reis's chair and a potted plant. "Perhaps we could collaborate, lift the hearts of our poor friends."

Reis wished at that moment they did have a clarinet in the case instead of a sniper rifle, an instrument of expression and love instead of death. There had been enough killing for one day. Reis remembered the black-clad mercenaries crumpling as they shot them, one by one; the blood everywhere as Edgar had fallen at their feet...

"Are you okay?" Teon asked, and Reis realized they hadn't answered the question.

"Yeah, sorry. I'm a pianist, actually. This clarinet... It's Edgar's." Reis mentally crossed their fingers, hoping Teon wouldn't want to see it.

"Are you dating Edgar?" Teon's eyes sparkled in the low hospital lighting, and Reis shifted in their chair. "An artistic soul, at that. Maybe Edgar's not lost to the music world yet."

"Teon, enough," the artist chimed in. "Don't embarrass Reis, or Edgar for that matter. Al and Glenn hated it when you used to do that."

"Teon's not embarrassing me," Reis said. They didn't want the conversation to end. They wanted to learn more about Edgar and his family from these kind, loving, interesting people. "I'm enjoying learning a little more about Edgar. He's not very forthcoming."

"Well, yeah," Teon sighed. "I dunno if it was because his dads toured all the time, but Edgar grew up to be a proper Anverite. We used to joke when Unification occurred he was finally in the right country. None of us were shocked when he decided to study programming at Anver University and move here permanently. Glenn was a bit heartbroken though. I think he'd always hoped, deep down in his heart, that his son would come around to love the arts. Instead, he left us all behind. Said we were an embarrassment. But that's all water under the bridge. Now he's in trouble and we're here because you can't push family away."

"I'm glad you came." Reis didn't know if Edgar would be happy to see these myriad faces, but surely being on the Killing Game's shitlist would make him glad for the support of family and friends. A pang of gentle jealousy and loneliness flowed through Reis's veins. What Reis would have given for a support structure like this one in recent years as their family fell away from them, and Edgar had thrown all this away.

He had to have his reasons, and they were none of Reis's business. Choosing to protect Edgar hadn't come from some sense of solidarity, but out of respect for Edgar's personhood. He didn't deserve to be treated like his life had no value. Nobody deserved that. Especially not in the cause of making a political point. The Killing Committee was no more than a band of terrorists, hell bent on destroying the peace patriots like Elias Torell had fought so long and hard for.

"Do you know why Edgar's here?" Reis asked. It seemed ridiculous they might not, and yet, even now, there were those who often didn't pick up on the cliques and memes inherent in Internet culture or chose to disregard them entirely. The mainstream media had a blanket ban on reporting on trolls, lest they become famous because of it. Picking up the Killing Game story while a target was active was as good as putting a bullet in their head.

"Not a clue," the artist said, putting down her sketchbook. "I'm Leah Mendes, by the way. She/her pronouns, if you would."

Reis nodded. "There's a site on the Dark Web called The Killing Game. Each month, a person is chosen at random to become a target. The first person to upload video showing the target being murdered will receive one million dollars in cryptocurrency and immunity from prosecution."

Teon's eyes widened, and he turned to Leah. "So that's what they were talking about..."

"Who?" Reis asked. "If you know something, you have to tell me!"

"Do we?" Leah shook her head, her eyes and stance full of caution. "How do we know you're not an assassin?"

"I wouldn't harm him!" Reis said. "I've sworn to protect him and get to the bottom of this Killing Game. I will find out who the perpetrators are and bring them to justice."

"Oh, so you're a cop?" Teon asked. "Explains why that clarinet case you're carrying is actually a gun case. You had me nervous there for a few, friend. I'd be heartbroken if I shared a song with a murderer." Teon bared their teeth, every part the protective figure when it came to Edgar.

"I'm not—" Reis opened their mouth to elaborate when the double doors opened, and a surgeon dressed in green scrubs emerged. Everything about his walk suggested exhaustion as he shuffled into the waiting room.

"The surgery was successful," the balding man announced. "Edgar's condition is serious, but stable. We were able to stop the bleeding and remove the bullet lodged in his large intestine."

The gathered crowd clapped, and Reis joined in, their drowned spirits lifting at the good news.

"Can we see him?" Teon asked.

"In a few minutes he'll be in recovery; we'll allow a few visitors then. After that, access will be restricted until visiting hours begin." The surgeon shuffled away, heading back into the operating room. Reis let out a long sigh of relief. Edgar had made it this far. Surely the universe wouldn't be so cruel as to have him survive the surgery, only to be killed by a greedy citizen? Reis looked around the room, wondering if any of these "friends" were foes in disguise. With how little they knew about Edgar, it was impossible to know for sure if they were sitting here talking to a clever hitman.

If there was a killer here, they would reveal themself in time. Reis stood and walked to the bathroom, eager to tidy up before going in to see Edgar. They walked into a stall and removed their binder, chest aching from the long hours of wearing it. They stuffed it in the gun case before dressing and exiting the stall. They walked to the bank of sinks and mirrors on the far wall where they dried their hair as best as they could with paper towels and started to tease out the knots. It was hard to comb their dank ringlets with only their fingers, but they worked at it until they felt vaguely presentable. Looking in the mirror showed a presentation that was more femme than they usually went for, but the low-level thrum of dysphoria wasn't enough to distract them today. They decided not to waste any more time and returned to the waiting area.

The Soulmates' fanboy receptionist was leading Teon, Leah, and the others into the recovery room when Reis emerged. Reis quickly merged into the group, fearing they'd be left out while these other, unverified strangers got access to Edgar's bedside. It would only take one slip of the hand to cut or bend an IV line, for a friend to become a killer, some hidden, microphone-sized camera capturing the grainy footage that would net them a million dollars.

But Reis was here. They'd made it back to Edgar's side, and despite their fears, Edgar had survived the greenhouse. They tried not to ruminate, but it was hard to see him lying in the bed, face ashen, and not feel like it was their fault. If they'd been a better shot; if they'd been watching Edgar more carefully... No. They were lucky to have survived at all against a squad of trained mercenaries. Next time they wouldn't be so lucky, and the Killing Committee was likely to send better assassins as the game lingered on without resolution. Without the power they so desperately craved—the power to destroy The Twin City-States from within, and tear Anver from Kasyova like two lovers whose courtship they disapproved of.

Reis was not going to let that happen. They stepped forward and took Edgar's hand in theirs, squeezing it gently.

"Edgar, it's okay. I'm here... I'm not going to let anything happen to you, I swear it..."

Chapter Seven

EDGAR

Edgar stirred. His vision was blurry, his senses fuzzy, and there was the sense of some distant pain he was unable to recall suffering. He tried to remember what had happened, but the knowledge remained stubbornly out of reach. Colorful blurry people surrounded him on all sides, and familiar scents reached his nose, igniting a strong sense of nostalgia that was more than welcome in this strange and uncertain moment. Wherever he was, he felt safe. Whoever these people were, they were people he knew and trusted.

"Edgar, it's okay. I'm here... I'm not going to let anything happen to you, I swear it..." A voice not rooted in nostalgia cut through the warm softness of his senses. This voice was good, possibly more welcome than all the others, and yet belonged to dangerous times. He remembered a shattered greenhouse, black-clad assassins, a broken-down flower shop... His memories came rushing back in a flood.

"Reis!" Edgar struggled to sit up and found himself tethered to the bed by a vast array of tubes. Gentle hands guided him back down, soothing him and urging him not to move. He concentrated on seeing, rubbing his eyes with the one hand that wasn't hooked up to an IV line. The room swam into focus, and he smiled when he saw Reis leaning over him with a concerned expression. Half a dozen figures from his extended creative family stood around the bed, each with a gratitude in their eyes to see him well he didn't feel worthy of. He'd let them all fall by the wayside after his fathers had died, never bothering to return the phone calls and birthday cards. Why were they here now, after all these years? There was Teon, his godparent; Leah, his surrogate mother; the backing singers Kristy and Ana. The Soulmates' manager and bodyguard Sebastian stood in the rear, looming over the whole scene like a strong and silent bouncer.

He almost felt guilty he'd called out for a person he'd known for three days instead of one of these other meaningful figures from his past. He cleared the cobwebs from his throat and played with his hospital bracelet, lost for words now he had everyone who loved him gathered in one room.

"I can't believe you all came... Thank you," Edgar managed, a little overwhelmed by it all. They looked at him with loving glances as though no time at all had passed, even though it had been years. He'd been so busy with his new life in Anver that he hadn't given them the time and care they deserved. After his fathers had died and they'd scattered to the four winds, he'd never known what to say. He knew he'd disappointed them by studying programming instead of the arts and moving to Anver, and it was a gulf he'd never been able to bridge with them, if only because he couldn't explain his reasoning.

Truth was, he was frightened of being heir to The Soulmates. His fathers had been extraordinary, loving people, and he was not. He'd never shown any affinity or talent at singing, stage acting, writing, or art, and the forthright nature of Kasyovans scared him a little at times. In Anver, people were more reserved. They kept their personal lives behind closed doors and presented a professional face to strangers. Edgar was fine with that. He preferred people not knowing who he was, because he didn't know who he was. He didn't want anyone else to know he was lost, empty, and a failure.

But now these people who all knew it were here, surrounding his bedside, claiming to still love him after all these years. It was too much. Why were they here? Why was Reis still here, protecting him like he meant something to them? Edgar was nothing, nobody. The only major surprise in his life had been that the Killing Game had even thought to target someone so absolutely insignificant in the grand scheme of things.

He wasn't going to let the Game hurt them too.

"I'd like to be alone, if you don't mind," Edgar said. The disappointed glances in their eyes stung like bees but pushing them away was—and had always been—the kindest thing to do. They had lives to go back to—families, careers, creative endeavors—whereas Edgar had nothing to lose. If he died, the papers would manage a one-line obituary about how the son of The Soulmates had come to a whole lot of nothing. Nobody would remember the business apps he'd written for faceless clients, the lines of code he'd churned out in his cubicle at Central Systems and later at home. His fathers were immortal, their voices heard around the world every day.

Edgar watched them shuffle out. All except for Reis, who stubbornly remained at his bedside. Their expression was a blank slate that Edgar couldn't read.

Edgar sighed, his chest constricting as he realized he needed to push Reis away for their own safety. "You should go, too, Reis. I can't ask you to protect me anymore."

"I don't recall you ever asking," Reis said, their voice soft and barely audible amidst the beeping of the heart monitor and the various machines whirring around them. "I chose this. I decided to help you."

"I still don't understand why. It's one thing to stop and help an injured person in the street, but quite another to stand back-to-back with someone in a shootout. You've done more than any Good Samaritan would be expected to. I'm grateful, but I should go alone from here."

"That's it? You're going to dismiss me?" Reis legitimately seemed hurt, and Edgar sighed, his stomach aching as he did so. He remembered the sensation of the bullets tearing through him, of bleeding out in Reis's arms. He'd made his peace with dying right there, in the arms of someone who cared. He didn't want Reis to leave, but how could he ask them to stay, knowing to do so would probably kill them?

"They're going to get me, Reis, one way or another. I didn't quite believe it before, but now I know they're coming for me and they won't stop until I'm dead. They won't care about the lives of the people I love, whether the rules will offer them immunity or not. The kind of people who would kill for a million dollars don't care about collateral damage. They would have mowed you down in an instant if you hadn't shot them first."

"I know." There was something feral about Reis's appearance, their hair hanging in disheveled ringlets, exhaustion haunting them, yet still a spark of determination flaring in their eyes. "I also know the second I walk out of this room, you're fair game to any nurse, orderly, or visitor who wants to slice your IV line or shoot air into your veins."

"I'm always going to be a target," Edgar explained. "I'll never have a moment's peace for the rest of my life. They're going to get me eventually—whether it be today, tomorrow, or the day after. I can't run from it any longer. I'm not even sure I should. It's not that I don't value my life, but who am I to ask you to lay down your life for mine? I've achieved very little in my time on this Earth. I haven't changed the world. I've done nothing for people to remember me by."

"Your friends seemed to disagree."

"They're not my friends. They're friends of my fathers—people I've disappointed over and over through the years. I love them, but we have nothing in common. I have no creative talents to speak of. I'm not destined to become an entertainment sensation or move the hearts of millions. I suppose they told you who my fathers were?" Edgar sighed. "You don't know what it's like to have famous parents. To live in their shadow day after day—to only be known as their child. The world's eyes ever upon you, wondering what you'll become. And then it turns out the only thing you're talented at is writing instructions for machines to follow."

"I understand better than you think." Reis smiled, shaking their head. "What if I told you my father was Elias Torell?"

"The Father of Unification?" Edgar's eyes widened. "Was? I didn't know he was dead."

"He's not—physically at least. But his mind is gone—stolen by dementia. He lives full-time in a facility, and I'm left with the same existential angst you are. Who am I? What have I done with my life to be worthy of the DNA running through my veins? Before I met you, I was just another person living in a rundown apartment, clinging to odd temp jobs to pay the bills. My mother and father are both gone. I had no direction, no purpose, and no way to find any. When Ash called me and told me about the Killing Game, of course I got involved. He played me like a fiddle, aware I was trying to fill a hole in my life. He knew I would never pass up the opportunity to be a saint and savior if it meant I could make waves in the ocean like my father." Reis scoffed and stood up. They paced the room as nurses walked in and flitted about Edgar, checking his vital signs. Reis waited until they moved along to the next patient to continue. "We're the same, Edgar. We're both searching for meaning in our lives."

"It's too late for me to find it. I'm a marked man. How long can I go on like this until someone kills me? Every second is borrowed time, and the clock's ticking, Reis. I wasted a lot of years in self-doubt and self-loathing, never even really understanding my life wasn't fully realized. Now I know there's a gap in my life, but I don't have time to fill it." Edgar closed his eyes. "I regret a lot of things I never made time for, but I can't change that now."

"You're still alive," Reis pointed out. "As long as you still draw breath, it's never too late. What do you want to do, Edgar? Do you want to live, or are you giving up because you can't be bothered to try?"

"I don't even know where to begin," Edgar admitted. "Until three days ago, I thought I was happy enough. My whole world's been turned on its head. I don't know what to do or what to think—whether I should invite people in or tell them to go away for their own protection. I'm scared, all the time."

"I'm scared too. You were shot right beside me. I felt so helpless, watching you bleed out and knowing there was nothing I could do but keep shooting. I held you close, and I thought that was it, I was going to lose you..." Reis turned their head away, in a vain attempt to hide the tears welling in their eyes.

"Reis. Look at me," Edgar commanded. He reached up and turned Reis's chin toward him, smiling as he witnessed a stray tear rolling down their cheek. He wiped it away with his thumb, cursing the tubes that kept him tied to the bed and the low-level pain in his gut when all he wanted to do was sit up and pull Reis down with him. He made himself content with watching Reis's brown eyes sparkle in the low light of the recovery room. This. This was meaningful, in a way nothing else in a long time had been. Reis's soft cheek beneath his hand. Reis's care and concern for his life. It reminded him of the soft ballads Al had loved; the crooners whose soft timbres often echoed through the apartment they'd called home for the longest time. He'd come home from school to find them dancing in the living room, swaying to the old crackle and warmth of vinyl records they refused to surrender in the digital age. Their lives were overflowing with meaning and purpose... How had he grown up to be so devoid of it once they'd gone and could no longer guide him? Yet here... Here was a feeling worth living for, if he only knew what to do with it, how to preserve it in crystal so it never turned to dust.

"Time to go." A nurse swooped in cheerfully and turned to Reis. "If you wait out in the hall, I'll let you know when your partner's settled in his room."

Reis nodded. With one last look at Edgar, they picked up their gun case, turned their back, and walked out of the room.

Chapter Eight

REIS

Reis sat in an empty waiting room. They felt the absence of Teon and Leah, wondering if Edgar's brusque dismissal would push them out of his life on a more permanent basis. They knew Edgar had done it for his extended family's safety and well-being, but Reis had felt a lot more secure with people they were learning to trust around them. They'd felt as though they could share the load, and now it was squarely back on their own two shoulders, Edgar's survival a burden Reis had to bear alone.

No, not a burden. Edgar's life was precious, and the responsibility of protecting it was an honor—but at the same time, it was terrifying to think Reis was the only one standing between Edgar and a world full of unknown assassins who could make an attempt on his life at any time. They longed for sleep but refused to let their eyes close until they were at Edgar's bedside. Then, with their ears wide open and their gun within arm's reach, they could afford the luxury of a guarded catnap.

Reis woke suddenly from a nightmare, horror spreading through their body as they realized they'd fallen asleep in the waiting room. Nobody had woken them with news.

Reis rushed to the reception desk, only to find it empty. The Soulmates' fanboy at the desk was gone. No doubt his shift had ended, and he'd left for the day. Reis started down the corridor, trying to remember where they'd wheeled Edgar's bed after they'd removed him from the recovery room. He looked through the window set in each door, searching for some sign of Edgar. Foolish. They'd been careless, allowing themself to fall asleep. How many hours had passed where Edgar had been left unprotected?

Reis stopped dead in the corridor. Something outside this particular room aroused their suspicions. Perhaps it was the housekeeping cart—who cleaned the rooms this early in the morning? No, it was possible there'd been an accident someone had needed to clean up—vomit and bed-wetting had to be common—but there was something else. The cart looked to be a mess, its contents scattered haphazardly, as though someone had been rifling through the contents in a hurry. Searching for something.

Reis backed up against the wall and set their gun case down. The rifle was of no use here, and they slid the pistol from their belt. Basic military training came back to them. They breached the entrance, slamming the door wide open with a boot to find the pink-haired receptionist looming over Edgar's IV equipment. They tossed a needle in the sharps trash.

"Stop right there!" Reis hissed. They kicked the door closed and moved in front of it, blocking the only exit. The receptionist greeted them with alarm which quickly seemed to turn to arrogance.

"You're too late," the receptionist said. "There's already poison in his IV fluids. He'll be dead soon. I only need to stick around long enough to get the footage. What, are you really going to shoot me? They'd put you away for murder. Maybe his, too, if they decide to pin the poison plot on you." They shook their head. "You could kill me and steal the footage, but I'm not the target... You'd still be on the hook for my death. Looks like checkmate for you, friend."

Reis assessed their options but had to admit the scene looked bad. Desperation clawed at their insides. Had they really come so far, said so much, only to have it end like this? The ghost of Edgar's touch still lingered on their cheeks, their tenderness awakening something inside them like a dying fire being rekindled. The need to protect him and the fragile, unnamed emotion they'd shared flared in their veins.

They fired. Their aim shot true, and the IV bag exploded, knocking the stand to the floor. The receptionist jumped, and the element of surprise gave Reis enough time to tackle them. Reis didn't want to hurt them, but time was of the essence. Reis reached up and grabbed a vase sitting on the nightstand. They cracked it against the side of the receptionist's head to stun them. Satisfied they were out cold, Reis crawled over to Edgar's side. They pulled out the needle and pressed the sheet hard against the back of Edgar's hand to stem the bleeding. Reis's heart hammered in their ears, but they knew they couldn't relax yet.

"Reis?" Edgar stirred.

"Hush," Reis soothed. "I need you to press down hard on this. I have to take care of something. Wait a few minutes and then call a nurse. Tell them you accidentally pulled out your IV and knocked the vase onto the floor. Make sure they replace the IV bag. That one's poisoned." Reis guided Edgar's free hand over to the sheet-covered wound and let go. Turning back to the receptionist, Reis was glad to find they were still unconscious. Knowing they didn't have much time, they scooped up the receptionist and slung them over their right shoulder. Reluctant to leave Edgar for one more moment but knowing they must, they headed out into the corridor and down to the elevator. The emergency room was two floors down, and they tapped their foot as they waited for the elevator, anxious the receptionist might wake up and give them a fight. The doors closed painfully slowly behind them, challenging Reis's patience.

The ER was quiet. Reis walked in and set the receptionist down on a gurney, flagging down a passing nurse. "I found them passed out in a patient's room," Reis explained. "It looks like they slipped and fell, hitting their head on the nightstand on the way down." The broken vase would cover their story. If there was any suspicion, it would be on the receptionist to explain exactly what they'd been doing in a patient's room in the middle of the night. Reis was going to imagine they didn't want to own up to attempted murder, so it was unlikely they would face assault charges. *Checkmate*, Reis thought with satisfaction, as they took the steps two at a time to return to Edgar's floor.

Nurses flocked to Edgar's room as Reis walked down the hallway. They hoped their cover story would fly. If they noticed the bullet embedded in the wall, the faint scent of gunpowder or the hole in the IV bag, the story would fall apart, but Reis hoped they weren't looking for reasons beyond the mundane. Also, they hoped the nurses didn't get together and discuss their cases in the break room, or the story would collapse. It had been the best Reis could manage at short notice. There had always been the truth, of course, but the Killing Game sounded so outlandish even to Reis's ears that a more believable lie had seemed less suspicious.

Reis waited again while the nurses cleaned up. They were beginning to hate the waiting room. Adrenaline made sitting down the last thing they wanted to do, and they paced like a caged lion, needing sleep, but knowing they were unlikely to find it even when they were close to Edgar again. One slip had brought them so close to the brink of disaster. Reis ran their fingers through their hair, wondering what was taking so long. What if some of the poison had made it into Edgar's blood? What if right now, he was convulsing and foaming at the mouth, dying an incomprehensible death right before the nurses' eyes?

The nurses left the room in a huddle. Reis walked back down the corridor and retrieved their gun case. It was thankfully still hidden behind the supply cart the receptionist had used as cover. Reis opened the door, grateful to see Edgar awake and alive.

Edgar smiled. "A rude awakening, I gotta say. I dreamed my bones were being pulled out through my skin, and I woke to some real-life pain. What the hell happened?"

"When I arrived here, there was a rather hostile receptionist who was obviously aware of the price on your head. I was too focused on other things to take them seriously as a threat. That, and... I fell asleep when they were preparing your room. I'm sorry. That was too close for comfort. They'd already injected your IV with poison... I had no choice but to rip it out."

"The loud noise? That was gunfire I heard, right? I was able to convince the nurses it was the sound of the vase smashing, though I don't know how well that'll hold up."

"Yeah. I'm surprised half the floor didn't come running. The receptionist had me in a spot. I shot the IV bag in hopes of destroying the poison. It also gave me the advantage—they were expecting me to freeze long enough to give them time to film your death." Reis stashed the gun case in a closet and slumped down in a chair. "I'm so tired, Edgar."

"I know. I'm sorry. You don't have to do this, Reis. You can go home, get some rest."

"You're not safe here. You can't even defend yourself at the moment. I'm not leaving you alone to get killed by some amateur with too many student loans." Reis closed their eyes and rubbed their temples, feeling a tension headache coming on. "I'm going to make this clear right now: no matter how much you beg and plead, no matter how tired or strung out I get, I'm not leaving you to die. If it hasn't penetrated your thick skull yet, I care about what happens to you. I don't know what that means right now but stop trying to push me away for my own good. I'm a grown adult, and I can make my own decisions. My choice is to stay by your side until you're safe."

"You're crazy, but I appreciate it," Edgar said. "Not that I'm in any position to argue if I did have a problem with it, but I don't. I can rest easy knowing I have a guardian angel watching over me."

Reis stood up and walked to the window. The neon lights of Anver glowed beneath them. This far up in the tower, the view was incredible, and they stood and drank it in until Edgar's breaths grew shallow and even, signaling he'd fallen back to sleep. The city seemed to be pulsing, aglow in technological glory. In the distance, the dimmer orange light of Kasyova stood out against the horizon. Elias Torell's legacy lived and breathed, a unified state that brought peace and prosperity to all.

"I'm no angel," Reis whispered to themself. "Just a misguided soul who's falling in love with you."

Chapter Nine

EDGAR

"Stretch, hold it... And down," Edgar's physical therapist instructed, and Edgar returned to a comfortable, relaxed, upright position. After weeks in bed, it was good to finally be up and about, even if the smallest of exercises tired him within minutes. Reis sat, one eye on a novel, another on Edgar, like a hawk watching for any signs of activity. With them there, Edgar was able to concentrate on healing and avoid thinking about the random strangers who could make an attempt on his life at any time.

In some ways, it seemed unfair to load another burden onto Reis, but they'd assured Edgar they wanted it that way, and so Edgar had relented. It wasn't so bad, having a bodyguard, especially one as attractive as Reis. Once Edgar started to heal, he'd started to really *notice* Reis—the way they moved, comfortable and confident in their own skin, regardless of whether they were wearing their binder. The two aspects within Reis seemed to seamlessly merge and blend to make one whole being— kind, sweet, and gentle one moment, fierce, assertive, and protective in the next.

Reis had filled him in on the events at the police station, and Edgar was looking forward to moving to a safe house within the next week. Reis had been in contact with the agents at the Bureau and scoped out the safe house for potential threats while Edgar was busy with appointments. They still weren't sleeping as much as they should, but the Bureau had seen fit to give Reis and Edgar a laptop and two smartphones which they could use to keep tabs on the Killing Game website. Edgar soon discovered Reis really liked cats, judging from their previous social media reposts, and reading, from the amount of books they seemed to consume in any given day. Edgar was ready to requisition the Bureau for an e-reader but figured since their involvement was on the down low, it would be a mistake to ask for indulgences. He wondered how Reis managed to concentrate on anything while they kept one eye firmly focused on Edgar the whole time.

Edgar was helped to the shower for the daily indignity of washing. It was the only place Reis never followed, and Edgar was kind of glad for it. He needed to keep some secrets from Reis, like the threats that had started coming to his phone.

Threats from Agent Grady.

Edgar had been torn when Grady had first contacted him. It was nice to talk to someone who wasn't Reis, and he didn't feel safe enough yet to call Teon, Leah, and the others and apologize for his behavior. He'd been lonely and had wanted to talk to someone about the things on his mind without worrying Reis. But then Grady had started flirting, and just like at Central Systems, things had gotten out of hand. Instead of shutting things down immediately, he'd let Grady send him a dick pic or two. Grady had wanted a return favor, and he'd declined, letting Grady down in a way he'd thought was gentle yet firm. Grady's response had been so swift and brutal it had taken Edgar's breath away.

> *I can collect on the bounty, you know. Reis is dumb enough to trust me. It would be so easy.*

Edgar had wanted to throw away the smartphone there and then but knew it would be a mistake. Without their contacts at the Bureau, they'd have nowhere to go once Edgar was discharged from the hospital—and he knew Reis wouldn't allow them to stay at the safe house knowing the risks. They'd be sitting ducks without anywhere to go, closed in a net where it would only be a matter of time before someone recognized him and tried to collect.

He'd sent a dick pic back to Grady against his better judgement, feeling dirty in a way he never had sharing his details with hookups before. That had been consensual. This was nothing less than blackmail, and he was caught in the spider's web with no way out. From there, it had been easy for Grady to blackmail him further.

> *I can always send the pics and our dirty little conversations to Reis. They'd be heartbroken. I think they like you.*

Vos had "conveniently" arrived to take Reis to scope out the safe house the very next day, and Edgar had found himself lying in bed with Grady's text messages up on his phone, demanding another picture. *Fuck this whole situation.* Edgar felt bitter about it in ways he hadn't before—his total lack of freedom, the fact fear was on him at every corner and he had no choice about anything in his life anymore. How he wanted to take Reis's hand, get in a car, and drive across the border, but even physical escape wouldn't free them from the fear that now owned them and made them slaves.

Was that what the Killing Committee wanted? For him to be afraid? If so, they were winning every day he still drew breath. Perhaps, he thought, in one particularly dark moment, death would be easier. He wouldn't have to worry about endangering Reis or hurting them emotionally. Reis would be free from the chains that shackled them to him. Reis would be able to see his smartphone and know what had happened immediately, and maybe the answers they squeezed out of Grady's squirming body at gunpoint would lead them to the real villains behind the curtains, the people pulling the strings behind the scenes.

Edgar sat in the bathroom before his shower, emptying his bowel to spare the nurse another round of hauling his ass to the restroom. Grady was obviously tracking him using the pinpoint GPS in his phone and didn't hesitate to text him once he reached the bathroom.

> *You're getting discharged tomorrow. You think you're healed enough now to take my dick in your mouth?*

> *Fuck off,* Edgar texted back, icy fear freezing the blood in his veins.

Stop playing hard to get and answer the question.

If you rip my stitches I'll be back in here again where I'll be harder for you to get to.

Fine, fine. Just remember you won't get by on that excuse forever. I'm pulling a lot of strings to get you this safe house. You'd better show your gratitude.

Edgar closed his eyes, rubbing his forehead and exhaling deeply. "I'm done," he called, and he stashed his cellphone in his robe as the nurse came in to help him stand. He was grateful he was able to take the rest of his shower in silence without his phone buzzing. Grady had what he wanted—control. Edgar was his, safety being the price of his silence.

He went back to his room and feigned tiredness, the will to speak with Reis diminished. How could he hold a conversation with Reis and pretend to be upbeat about the safe house when they were just moving from the hospital to a smaller prison? His chest ached, longing to tell Reis what had happened, but knowing the truth would endanger them both. He clung to the thought he'd had earlier of Reis holding Grady at gunpoint, eyes shining with fury so pure it could blot out a million suns, and took some comfort in it. Grady would get what was coming to him. It was only a matter of time. As soon as he could break free from his net, he would. He'd tell Reis and let them decide what to do, and only hope and pray Reis would be able to look them in the eye once Grady sent them pictures of Edgar being used and abused.

Edgar sighed as they pulled up to the safe house. The apartment was in Kasyova, of all places, and Edgar felt both terror and trepidation at being home again. The apartment sat above a pub, which they walked through now. The traditional wooden bar was well-stocked with drinks, and Edgar knew he might end up down here a few times to drown his sorrows if things got worse. Faux lanterns lined the staircase, casting the upstairs hallway in a warm glow. The bare floorboards creaked as Grady unlocked the door and led them inside.

The inside was as traditionally Kasyovan as the downstairs, gaudy and grand, with a thick pile burgundy carpet and overbearing Paisley wallpaper. Details on the ceiling were picked out in gold leaf.

"This is some place!" Reis remarked, eyes wide with awe. "I've never seen anything like it, only in movies."

"Really?" Edgar asked. "My fathers' apartment looked kind of similar to this. It's quite a throwback." Edgar shuffled along the carpet, his walking frame getting stuck in the thick carpet. Despite the warm memories he associated with Kasyovan style and architecture, he longed for the modern simplicity of his apartment in Anver—all geometric shapes and sharp angles, decorated in pastel colors.

Maybe his distaste had more to do with the price he was paying for it. Grady lingered overlong helping Edgar into the chair, and he had to fight the urge to shake him off. It wouldn't do to poke the bear. It would only end in another round of threats to assert his dominance and control over Edgar. No, it was wise to let him think he was winning, for now. The severity of his injuries would buy him time in which to take action, and by the time they were healed enough for Grady to seriously approach him, he hoped he'd be on the run with Reis, the Twin City-States firmly in the rearview mirror. He didn't relish leaving everything he knew behind, but it had to be better than being hunted at every turn, being used and abused and kicked down.

He never expected to feel absolutely safe again, but he hoped there would be a time when the threats didn't come so thick and fast. Maybe then he'd be able to explore his feelings for Reis, go back to the warmth he'd felt the night he'd been admitted to the hospital to find Reis leaning over him with tears in their eyes. Edgar hated Grady more than anything for the wedge he'd driven between them, a separation driven by secrets and lies. It was easier to let the conversation lapse than risk the truth spilling out of him like vomit in a moment of weakness.

They had no other realistic options. Edgar had to remind himself of that fact over and over again as Vos outlined the safety and privacy features of the apartment. The place may have looked traditional, but it was packed to the rafters with modern technology that would keep an eye on their vital signs and wellbeing. Of course, those same features could turn the whole thing into a handy trap for someone like Grady. All he had to do was kill Edgar and steal the footage, and he'd be home free and a million dollars richer to boot. Ultimately, that had to be his goal, even if he was content to use and abuse Edgar for now. Edgar knew he couldn't fool himself into believing he was actually safe here, or he'd find a knife in his back.

"Give us a call if you need anything," Agent Vos said. "We're limited in the assistance we can provide, but we'll do our best to help you."

"Thank you," Reis said. Vos and Grady left, closing the door behind them and plunging the room into an awkward silence.

Edgar had to fight the overwhelming desire to spill the truth right then and there, but the cameras had him in a tighter web. If he confessed to Reis, Grady would know and move his calendar up to the killing phase. Who knew what traps he'd set in the apartment for precisely that eventuality? A small canister of toxic gas could take them both out without alerting anyone, and it would be easy to pin it on some faceless assassin while pocketing the money.

"Finally, we can relax a little." Reis smiled. "I can't wait to get a good night's sleep. I've been running on fumes for so long I don't think I even remember what it feels like to be fully rested."

"We can't afford to let our guard down too much," Edgar replied. "This isn't a permanent solution. We can't expect to live on the government's dime forever. Eventually we're going to have to decide what to do in the long run."

"Of course," Reis said. "Don't worry, I'm working on a plan. But right now, I'm going to take a nap." They walked into their room, leaving Edgar alone with his dark thoughts. His phone buzzed, and he swallowed the inevitable dread and pulled out his phone.

I can see you, Grady's text read.

Edgar closed his eyes and let out a long sigh, wishing for sleep to take him into oblivion. It took a while, but he eventually dozed off in the chair, losing himself in some blissful dream he couldn't remember upon waking.

Chapter Ten

REIS

Reis had noticed a change. A distance had sprung up between them, beginning sometime during Edgar's stay in the hospital. Now, they lay awake thinking about it, rolling over in the satin sheets as they considered a harsh thought. Edgar yelled from the other room. He did that a lot; nightmares, Reis presumed. They often thought about going into Edgar's room, but was afraid of what they'd find there. Would Edgar punish the intrusion into his private space? Or would Reis's care for Edgar pull them into his darkness?

Could it be Edgar didn't want them in his life anymore? They rolled the thought over and over, trying to see it from all angles. It wasn't as if Edgar had become brusque or unpleasant, but the tension that had grown between them seemed to have frozen over. It wasn't gone, per se, but it hadn't grown, as if it was being preserved in stasis for some indeterminate future time. Perhaps Edgar simply couldn't face starting a relationship when his future was so uncertain and volatile? That could be it, Reis thought.

But there was something else too. An undercurrent of anxiety coming from Edgar's direction. Reis had thought it was the fear of knowing he was being hunted, yet it shouldn't have grown as they came closer to Edgar's discharge. Edgar had never been so tightly wound as he was now that they were at the safe house. Even the most minor problems seemed to make him irritable. Cabin fever? Maybe, but Reis felt it was more than that. Something was keeping Edgar up at night. Something on his phone, from the way he often glanced down at it furtively. Could someone be texting him? Who would know the number? Had he done something stupid like start a social media account and given out his number to someone? Surely, he wouldn't be that dumb, given the situation he was in.

All Reis could do was wait and see. They had the freedom to leave the apartment, but rarely used it. Edgar seemed to get anxious when they wanted to go out, and it seemed unfair. They had their groceries delivered, Edgar hiding in his room when the driver came. Reis was feeling more than a little housebound as well, but they bore it as a necessity.

*

They sat watching television, late at night a couple of weeks into their self-imposed house arrest, when Edgar suddenly dropped his phone. Reis watched him pick it up, his face pale, palms clearly sweaty despite the cold. His momentary surprise only lasted an instant, but Reis caught it, and they knew the look. Fear. Someone was using the phone to threaten Edgar.

It had to be Grady or Vos. The thought struck Reis like lightning, and they almost bolted out of their seat before holding back. Of course, it all made sense. The cameras. The monitoring. This wasn't a safe house—it was a *prison*. A prison keeping Edgar alive until they had what they needed and could kill him, using the footage to collect the bounty. It was so perfect Reis kicked themself for not seeing it before. Of course, Edgar was being quiet. He was being manipulated behind the scenes. He was being twisted against Reis—but for what purpose? Reis had to know, and to know he had to get to the truth.

"I have to go out," Reis said. "The delivery driver was out of...things I need last time I ordered, and I need to get them."

"What kind of things?" Edgar asked. "If you're only going to the corner store, I can come with you. I really could use some fresh air."

"Do I really have to say it?" Reis snapped. They hated speaking to Edgar this way, but it was imperative he not nag to go outside, not today. All Reis needed was five minutes and they'd be back, ready to face Edgar about what was going on. "I need hygiene products. I'm not on hormones. I still have a menstrual cycle." They hated saying it out loud, which only made it more believable. They'd apologize to Edgar later, once the secret was out. Once they knew what strings Grady and Vos were tugging on to get Edgar right where they wanted him. They hated using gender dysphoria to manipulate anyone, but in this case, it was the easiest and most effective way to get the job done. Sometimes, life required ruthlessness, but they hated how much of that side they'd needed to tap into in recent times.

"I'm sorry." Edgar shook his head. "I didn't mean to pry into your personal life." He sat down, contrite, as Reis convincingly slammed the door.

Out in the hallway, Reis looked around for a breaker box. It might be downstairs in the pub, or even in the basement, which might be a problem if the owner was there cleaning the bar, as she often was out of hours. Thankfully, when Reis tiptoed downstairs, they found no signs of life. Hoping there were no cameras around, they looked in the cupboard under the stairs and hit gold. From there, it was a simple matter of pulling down the handle to turn off the main breaker. Reis realized how easy it would be for an assassin to do the same thing and resolved to ask the owner to put a lock on it once their tampering was discovered.

They thought about waiting a couple of minutes to make the store story more convincing and realized being caught in a lie was the least of their worries. If Grady and Vos came hustling down as soon as they realized the cameras and recorders were out, Reis would never get to find out what was happening in the secret world of Edgar's phone. They fumbled in the darkness, climbing the steps with painful slowness. They unlocked the door at the end of the hallway and let themself in.

"Stop!" Edgar called out. "I'm armed and I will shoot you!"

"It's me," Reis yelled. "This isn't an attack. I needed to talk to you without the cameras. We don't have long before someone realizes the surveillance system is out, so we need to work fast. Is it Grady or Vos?"

"What do you mean?" Edgar asked.

"Someone's threatening you via your phone. Your entire demeanor has changed the past few weeks. You're not stupid enough to hand out the number to that phone, which means the only people who know it are Grady and

Vos. It's a setup, isn't it? They're threatening you somehow. When they've gotten what they want, they'll kill you and use the footage to claim the reward. You haven't been able to tell me because they can hear and see every move we make."

"You're sharp," Edgar said. "Probably why I've lived this long. It's Grady. He started texting me when I was in the hospital. Made out like he was my friend and wanted to lend me an ear, until he started sending me pictures of his dick. I had to send him mine. He threatened to kill me if I didn't. From there, it was easy for him to use you against me. He promised to send you the sexts he made me send. I didn't want you to think..." Edgar used his phone to light up the darkness. "He used me, and once I realized the full extent of the trap, it was too late to escape it..."

"Why do I feel like there's more?"

"He threatened to make me perform oral sex on him once my wounds are healed."

"I'm going to fucking *murder* him. No, murder is too good. I'm going to torture him and make him plead for mercy. I trusted that son of a bitch. I trusted him!" Reis's heart pounded in their ears, spots hounding their vision.

"Reis." Edgar's hand on their shoulder jolted them back to reality. "Grady and Vos will be here in minutes. What's the plan? Stay or go?"

Reis swallowed their feelings, trying to focus on the moment. Edgar was right. They could extract vengeance later. For now, they needed to make a choice.

"We can't keep running," Reis said. "Eventually we'll get caught. We have to get to the heart of the matter.

Expose the identities of the Killing Committee members and take down the Game if you're ever going to be free. If Grady's working for them, he won't be dumb enough to bring his partner. Perhaps we can ambush him and extract some information."

"Grady's a Bureau agent," Edgar warned. "If we hurt him, we won't just be running from the Killing Game but from the government as well."

"If Grady and Vos told me any nuggets of truth, it's that the Killing Game conspiracy extends up to the highest-ranking echelons of the government. It was foolish of me to think Bureau agents could truly be on our side," Reis said. "This is the best lead we have, Edgar. We have to take it."

"Okay. Either side of the door, then? Tackle him when he comes through?"

"Yeah," Reis confirmed. They took their position and then shone the flashlight to illuminate Edgar's path on the other. They shone the flashlight over Edgar's face, catching a brief, brave-faced smile. Reis clicked off the flashlight and waited, breathing shallow breaths in hopes Grady wouldn't hear them lying in wait. Minutes passed, but to Reis it felt like hours, time slowing down to a crawl as they waited for a kettle that might never boil.

Grady had to come, didn't he? He wouldn't be able to steer clear believing someone else beat him to the kill. But then, if he truly knew something, if he was part of the Game, he wouldn't be a player now, would he? He could send any assassin up in the dark to make sure the deed was done and the Killing Committee got their point across.

Reis was about to voice their concerns to Edgar when a low click sounded, followed by a barely audible hiss. Was someone here already? Had the assassin used some other entrance, a window perhaps, to enter the apartment? Reis scanned the darkness, but it was impossible to see anything in the penetrating gloom. With no windows in the living room, there wasn't even a shard of moonlight to cast a shadow. If someone was in here with them, they'd have no chance, especially if the assassin had thought to wear night-vision goggles. Had Reis done the assassin's work for them by tripping the breaker? Had a killer been scoping out the building and chanced upon the perfect time to strike?

Reis's mind started to grow cloudy and exhausted. They felt more tired than they had the night Edgar was shot, trying to keep exhaustion at bay in the waiting room.

"Edgar..." Reis called out, sensing something was horribly wrong. In response, they heard Edgar slump to the ground. Gas. It had to be gas. Whether it was Grady flooding the apartment as some sort of contingency plan or a would-be assassin ensuring they didn't put up a fight, Reis knew they were in trouble. They covered their nose and mouth with their sweatshirt, trying desperately to stave off the sleeping gas, but it was too late. They lay close to the ground, crawling, trying to reach Edgar, but the pull of oblivion was too strong, and they sank down into the darkness.

*

Click. Voices. *Click click.* The sound of people talking and cameras flashing broke through the darkness as Reis stirred. The first thing they felt was the shag pile carpet beneath their fingers and a deep pounding in their skull.

"They're coming around." Grady's voice. Reis felt a distant sense of panic. Perhaps they should keep their eyes closed? But something was wrong, very wrong, in the way the voices in the background spoke in hushed tones. There was a smell in the air, a stench that took Reis back to childhood, to the civil war.

They recognized the smell of blood as a wave of fear threatened to make them vomit.

"Come on, sleepyhead. Wake up." Grady shook Reis, and Reis resisted the urge to shake him off after Edgar's revelations. If they hadn't felt so weak, it wouldn't have taken much to sit up and punch him while he least expected it, but Reis's arms and legs were heavier than lead. They opened their eyes, closing them again as the world spun in a blur. No, it wasn't wise to open them just yet. Instead, they worked on crawling to a sitting position, moving their knees under them and using the wall as support to maintain themself upright. Once they'd achieved that without too much nausea, they opened their eyes. They couldn't make much sense of the blurred shapes in front of them. Reis rubbed their eyes, and the sight before them took shape.

Blood. There was blood everywhere. Reis traced the trail across the floor with their eyes and looked up to the body pinned to the wall. Horror swept through them as they looked up to the ashen face, long hair swept in front of it... It was unmistakably Edgar.

The sound that came out of their mouth was something between a scream and a wail, a release of emotion so desperate Grady backed up. Reis got to their feet and grabbed Grady. They thrust him against the wall with enough force to knock the wind out of him, despite the pain in their arms and legs.

Nothing mattered anymore. Edgar was dead. All of Reis's efforts had been for nothing and killing this sack of shit would achieve nothing except letting off some steam.

"Why are you angry at me?" Grady asked. "I didn't do this." The corner of his lips twitched, the start of a smile that made Reis want to pound his face into pulp. "You did this, Reis. You even uploaded the video evidence to the Killing Game website. I guess that makes you the winner. Congratulations, Reis Asher. You played the long game, but you gained Edgar's trust and got him in just the right situation to kill him. He didn't even know what hit him."

"What?" Reis looked around, confused. "What the fuck? I didn't—I *wouldn't*—I was—"

"I have to take you into custody until the video is authenticated and your immunity confirmed, but honestly, it's mostly for your own protection. Some Soulmates fans are going to be upset you killed their only child."

"I didn't kill him!" Reis screamed. "I would never hurt him! This is a setup! I was knocked out!" They wrapped their hands around Grady's throat and squeezed. Two officers grabbed Reis from behind, pulling them off Grady, who only smiled, coughed, rubbed his throat a little, and proceeded to adjust his tie.

"You only gain immunity for killing him," Grady said. He walked past Reis with a smug grin on his face.

Reis struggled against the police officers as they cuffed them. Grady casually walked up to Edgar's body. "I don't know why you felt the need to put him on display, but I'm sure the video will make it all clear."

"There is no video because I. Didn't. Do. It." Reis spat in Grady's direction.

"Don't act so repulsed. You've killed before. Why is this so different? Because you knew him? Because he wasn't some faceless, masked intruder you gunned down in cold blood?" Grady shook his head. "It'll make headlines, Reis. Elias Torrell's child, a murderer. Such has been the influence of decadent Kasyovan culture that even the child of an upstanding citizen has been corrupted." Grady brushed the hair out of Edgar's eyes, revealing a blank, fixed stare. Those beautiful brown eyes would never see again. He was gone. Edgar had been the center of Reis's world, the one person they would have given everything to protect, but they'd never been able to tell Edgar that. The timing had never been right to say the words, and now they'd never have the chance.

Reis started to sob. They hated showing weakness, especially here in front of Grady, but it felt like a light had been permanently switched off in their brain. For three short weeks, their life had meaning and purpose. They'd cared about someone and it had given the world a little more light, a point. The things they'd taken for granted had seemed novel all of a sudden. The taste had been sweeter, somehow.

Now, Edgar was pinned to a wall with a bunch of nails in a horrific, ritual killing. Reis took a good, long, last look. His throat had been slit; his body nailed to the wall with a nail gun that still lay at the scene of the crime. He had to have been asleep, right? He probably hadn't suffered. He would have bled out quickly. But he was *gone*, all the same, his soul extinguished before he had even found his reason and purpose to live.

"Can I waive immunity?" Reis asked. "I don't want to be off the hook. Put me to death. Execute me. I don't want to live."

"Don't be stupid," Grady said. "The million will make you comfortable for the rest of your life. A show trial would serve no purpose. Edgar will stay dead no matter what you do."

"I will get you, Grady. I know you're on the Killing Committee. I will hunt you down and make your life a living hell for what you've done here. But don't think I'll shoot you down or slit your throat while you sleep. It's going to be a long, painful death for you."

"You really *are* stupid, aren't you? Whatever. Cool down in the tank and when they let you out, go the fuck home and stay out of shit that doesn't involve you." Grady waved his hand and the police led Reis away. Reis went willingly, the strength to fight ebbing out of him. There was no reason to fight these police officers. There was no reason to do anything at all, really. All they wanted was to go somewhere and sleep forever, to join Edgar in sweet oblivion.

A dozen camera flashes went off as they left the building, the media swarming the apartment block as soon as they'd gotten word. A hundred questions flew above Reis's ears and they ignored them all. It didn't matter what they said. Nobody would believe they hadn't killed Edgar. In the eyes of the world, Elias Torell's child was a murderer who had hunted and killed a man for money and fame.

They let themself be hustled into the back of a police car, which sped away from the melee at breakneck speed. The officers in the front said nothing, and Reis stared out of the window, trying to put together the pieces of what might have happened. Grady had flooded the apartment with sleeping gas, arrived on the scene, and killed Edgar before stringing him up for maximum effect. Somehow, he'd produced a video that showed Reis committing the act and submitted it in their name. As a discredited killer, nobody would ever believe a word Reis had to say again. They were out of the way of the Killing Committee's plan to destabilize the Twin City-States. Check and checkmate.

And Edgar was gone. Dead. Reis couldn't even begin to stare into the chasm of their heart. Their stomach lurched when they tapped into their memories of Edgar. They regretted so much about the past few weeks. Especially the time wasted in the apartment, where they'd felt too nervous to comfort Edgar and had maintained a respectful distance. Maybe if they'd played their cards differently, Edgar would still be alive. Maybe they'd have more than the memory of Edgar wiping away one stray tear with their thumb to last a lifetime.

There was no point ruminating on what might have been. Only what to do next. Vengeance burned in Reis's veins, a blood call beckoning them to take Grady to a place worse than Hell. They had to honor Edgar's memory, and killing Grady was a good start. Not that vengeance would end there. This tragedy would continue so long as the Killing Committee still existed. The Killing Game had to end, and Reis would not rest until each and every member of the Killing Committee was lying in a pool of their own blood, their plan in tatters.

Intermissions

Killing Committee Statement: 10:10pm, Friday August 3rd:

> *We are happy to announce the winner of the nineteenth Killing Game, Reis Asher (25), who will pocket the one million in cryptocurrency and immunity from prosecution for the murder of the target, one Edgar Tobias (29), carried out in the late hours of Thursday August 2 and attested to in the video evidence presented below:*

> *[x]*

> *Text description of video for the visually impaired: Night vision camera captures Reis Asher grabbing Edgar Tobias from behind in a chokehold and slashing his throat. Asher drags the body to the wall and nails it to the wall with a nail gun. They linger for a moment, kissing the corpse on the mouth, and then sit on the floor and proceed to wait for the police to arrive, where they fall asleep [end of video].*

As of this posting, the Killing Game is concluded, and no new targets are planned.

We think we've had enough fun. Now the real game begins.

Are you ready?

Chapter Eleven

EDGAR

Edgar gasped and took a deep breath, waking suddenly from a nightmare so intense he could have been sure it was reality. He coughed, realizing his throat was parched. He couldn't see a thing. It became apparent from the weight and sensation on his face he was wearing a blindfold.

He tried to move his arms, only to find with a rising sense of panic that he was handcuffed to a bed. He struggled against the cuffs, but they held firm, scraping against the metal bed frame.

"You're not going to break those chains, Ed, so don't even try."

"Grady." Edgar could barely spit out the name. His voice sounded hoarse and alien, even to his own ears, and there was a strange taste in his mouth. A pit of fear opened inside him when he thought about Reis and he grit his teeth to steady himself. "Where's Reis?"

In response, he felt an intrusion at his lips, cold and sterile. He recognized it as a drinking glass and let it pass. The water soothed his mouth and throat, making it easier to talk. Grady stepped away and set the drink down with the "tink" sound of glass on glass. His footfalls came closer again and Edgar felt the warmth of Grady's breath on his face as he reached around to untie the blindfold. The room was well lit, with black walls and a tiled floor. A window was set into the wall, but Edgar couldn't see out of it.

"Where am I?" Edgar asked.

"A maximum-security cell in the basement of the Bureau. Nobody will think to look for you here. I'll have you all to myself for as long as I want you." Grady smiled with too many teeth, and Edgar wished he could mess up that grin by planting his fist in it.

"You still haven't answered my question from before. Where's Reis?"

Grady reached for the table, grabbed a remote, and flicked on a flat-panel television set up in the corner of the room. A media circus overwhelmed the steps in front of the safe house as three officers led Reis away. "ELIAS TORELL'S CHILD REIS ASHER ACCUSED OF MURDER" the headline read. The sub-headline was even more chilling: "*Asher collects one million in Killing Game Prize.*"

"Reis is enjoying their newfound fame for killing you," Grady explained. "The murder scene was rather grisly. I'm proud of it. It wasn't easy to put together, but it does tie up some loose ends rather neatly. The world thinks Edgar Tobias is dead, that annoying brat will take the million and shut up, the Killing Committee has achieved the media coverage they wanted, and I get you all to myself."

"If you think Reis will take the money and run, you're sadly mistaken. Reis won't give up looking for me."

"Reis thinks you're *dead*, Edgar. They saw your body, throat slit, hanging from the wall of the apartment. They have no leads on the Killing Committee, and the media will hound them until their dying day, so happy that Elias Torell's only child fell from grace. Tensions are already flaring between Kasyovans and Anverites due to the murder. It's exactly what the Committee wanted from the Killing Game. You played your roles perfectly."

"Fuck you," Edgar spat. He tugged at the cuffs, but they didn't budge.

"Good luck getting out of those. I'll let you go when you comply like the good little slave you're going to be. You're dead, Ed. You have no name; your national insurance number has been closed. You're a non-person. Deceased. Records deleted. You've ceased to exist, except here in this basement. I'm your master now. You'll kneel and lick my boots; you'll service me, and you'll love it." Grady grinned.

"You might as well kill me now. I'll never serve you."

"You will, in time. Once I've broken your spirit, you'll be able to come home with me. Reis may have gotten a million dollars, but I have something far more exquisite for my troubles. I can't wait to see you bobbing on my cock of your own free will. Christ, it's making me hard just thinking about it."

"You'd destroy the Twin City-States to indulge your perversion? You're sick in the head, Grady."

"No, you were a bonus. I do believe in the cause. Anver and Kasyova were never meant to be united. Anver is slowly being corrupted by Kasyovan influence. We used to be world leaders in technology, but now our children flee to the arts. Programmers and mathematicians are becoming musicians and playwrights, self-indulgent little pests consuming the world's resources while science and medicine falls by the wayside. Anver used to be number one in the world for medical advancements. Now we're tenth."

"Yeah, you're right. Anverite doctors no longer have to worry about prosthetic limb replacements now people aren't blowing themselves up in a petty, meaningless civil war," Edgar interjected. "But I suppose arms dealers and medical companies don't make their fortunes from human happiness like artists do."

"Funny, coming from a man who fled his arts heritage for the world of computers. I thought you understood what was going on here."

"What I understand is I'm chained up, after weeks of being on the run from my killers, chosen by a group of people I never knew existed to become the sacrificial lamb for a cause I don't believe in. All I wanted was to live a normal life, Grady. I never wanted any of this."

"You wish you'd never met Reis, then? You'd like to turn back the clock and pretend none of this ever happened? Be back in your apartment, calling Chris every time he broke something so the pair of you could have a little human interaction? Maybe you'd have ended up in bed with him eventually, and you'd have fallen in together like so many couples do. Going through the motions... Marriage, children, career... That's it? That's what you wanted?"

"There's nothing wrong with that," Edgar protested. "You don't need to stand out in order to matter. The world needs ordinary people just as much as it needs people like my fathers. Someone has to keep the world running. I was fine with it."

"Until you met Reis," Grady snarled.

"Until I met Reis," Edgar admitted. "Something changed and I realized I wanted more from my life. I wanted to feel like I felt with them. Alive. When the bullets lodged themselves in my stomach and Reis held me in their arms, I thought I could die right then and be happy. I thought 'this is what it's like to be loved—really loved.'" Edgar closed his eyes. Why was he telling Grady, of all people, this private, personal detail about himself? This confession was unfolding to himself at the same time he was telling it to Grady. Reis had some essential spark that made his life feel like it mattered. He wanted to protect that spark, foster it, and watch it grow. He wanted to boost Reis to their full potential as the exceptional person they were.

"You're in love with them. Figures." Grady shrugged. "Or what you think of as love, anyway. It's really Stockholm syndrome. You were destined to fall in love with them. Trapped in close quarters as you were, under threat of death. Who wouldn't love the person who promised to keep them safe? It's okay. I can replicate the same effect here. Soon, you'll depend on me for everything. You'll need me, Edgar. You'll love me and forget about Reis."

"That'll never happen," Edgar said.

"You'll see. I'll leave the television on for you, so you can watch Reis's downfall. I find it all so very entertaining. They thought they were an angel, swooping in to save an innocent life. Now their wings are black, their reputation sullied." Grady walked to the door, opened it, and stepped outside. Edgar heard the beep and click of the electronic lock engaging, and closed his eyes, fighting back a deep despair that threatened to overwhelm him. Grady had won. The Killing Committee had won. How foolish had they been to think they could beat such powerful people? Both he and Reis had been crushed beneath the heel of an overpowering foe, and now only lived to amuse the people who they had dared to defy.

Chapter Twelve

REIS

Reis stood in the ruins of the florist shop, wondering why they were here. It was silent, like before—a welcome relief from the media circus that had been following them nonstop since they'd been arrested and subsequently released without charge.

The system was broken if such a thing could actually be allowed to happen, but it had. Reis had been handed the password to an online wallet full of cryptocurrency and set loose on the world. The people of Anver didn't even seem fussed that Reis had gotten away with murder. It was part of the Game honoring their agreement, people seemed to be saying. Like a contract.

But a contract killing was still a killing. There was no way they should have been allowed to leave the police station under some declaration of immunity, and yet it had happened. If Reis had needed proof the Killing Committee conspiracy went all the way to the top, they now had it. Even the President of the Twin City-States had mumbled through an apology and promised an investigation on why and how immunity papers had been prepared. Reis expected they had him by the balls. They probably had some tasty morsel to blackmail him with, and nothing would ever be done about the killers walking free. Nineteen murders. Nineteen perpetrators, all free.

The world was broken. The illusion of a perfect, united, free Twin City-States as their father had longed to create lay shattered at their feet. It was a dream lost to time and corruption, twisted by the blackened hearts of humankind.

Unrest was already brewing. Kasyovans were heartbroken and furious that Reis had been allowed to walk free—indeed, that the Killing Game had been allowed to happen at all and had targeted the son of two beloved Kasyovan celebrities. They saw it as an affront to their culture by Anverites eager to disrupt the status quo. Anverite businesses in Kasyova were being attacked and looted, with Anverties attacked in the street and told to "go home" like the "ungrateful scum" they were. K-City Radio talking heads ranted on about how they'd saved Anver from itself, only to be repaid in the worst way.

Broken glass crunched beneath the soles of Reis's boots as they headed out into the greenhouse. The bodies were gone, of course, but traces of their blood remained. Reis knelt at the spot where Edgar had fallen. His bloodstain was brown and faded, but still there. Reis reached out and touched it, closing their eyes.

All their efforts, all their travails, had been for nothing. Reis had fought with all their might, only to lose Edgar in the end, and only this bloodstain served as a marker that they'd ever met. They'd thought they'd lost him then, and Edgar had been smiling—smiling!—even as his lifeblood seeped out onto the concrete floor. His brown eyes had been wide as saucers as Reis had held his fragile body, willing him to stay alive.

Now the whole world thought Reis had killed him. Even Reis wasn't too sure anymore. When they'd awoken on the floor, it had seemed obvious Grady was responsible for Edgar's death, but now, with every finger in the Twin City-States pointed directly at them, the truth became blurry and unreal. They'd seen the video on a laptop computer brought to the interrogation room at the station. It was Reis in the video, grabbing Edgar from behind and slitting his throat. Reis who dragged him across the floor, who nailed him to the wall like some kind of ritual sacrifice.

It wasn't possible, Reis reminded themself. No mind control, hypnotism, nothing could make them harm a hair on Edgar's head. Obviously, a good video editor had used face-mapping technology to paste their face onto that of the real perpetrator. Grady had probably sent someone of a similar height and build for exactly that reason. It was a good fake, but it *was* fake. The Killing Committee had only accepted it because they'd wanted to. They were the ones who'd commissioned it. Reis being the killer solved all their problems—the embarrassment of the target eluding their decree was mitigated, and both the identity of the target and the killer aroused a media whirlwind along ethnic and cultural fault lines.

Nobody seemed to care that Edgar was dead, not really. Not Edgar the person. Just Edgar the son of The Soulmates, Edgar the celebrity child, Edgar the subject of a hit single. None of the obituaries cared he was a computer programmer, he was bisexual, he had handsome brown hair and soft brown eyes and a smile to die for. Only Reis cared about those things, but Reis wasn't allowed to speak up. The world had already decided they were Edgar's killer, and nothing—not even the truth—would clear their name. There would always be those who believed Reis had slaughtered the man they'd sworn to protect in the most cynical back stab of all time.

Reis opened their backpack and took out their cellphone. Grady had confiscated it when they'd moved into the safe house, and it had been returned to Reis upon receipt of the Prize. It was a little chipped, but it still worked. They looked up Teon Escher's number in a search engine, marveling at how easy it was to find every detail about them and their recording studio.

It would be dumb to call, Reis told themself. Reis was the last person Teon would want to hear from in a million years. How hurtful would it be to get a phone call from Edgar's killer protesting their innocence? Yet who else could possibly listen? Ash was no longer anything resembling a friend. If Reis marched up to their father's bedside, their father would likely believe them, only to forget the moment Reis left the room. Reis needed someone to believe in their innocence. They only hoped they'd made enough of an impression on Teon that it might be possible to convince them.

Reis turned the cellphone over in their hand. What did they have to lose, really? Would it be so bad if Teon hung up on them? With that thought in mind and their heart in their mouth, they made the call.

"Hello?" Teon's voice sounded heavy and distraught.

"I need you to listen. Don't hang up. Please."

"Who is this?" Teon asked, outrage seeping into their voice. "Reis? Reis fucking Asher? How *dare—*"

"I didn't kill him!" Reis nearly screamed their statement into the microphone. They stifled a sob. "I would have died sooner than hurt Edgar. You have to believe me! It's a setup!"

"Funny, because from where I'm standing, it sure don't look like you handed back that million bucks. Looks like you're sitting pretty on my godson's blood money."

"I only kept it because I need it to find out who's behind the Killing Game. I need to bring them to justice, Teon, and I need your help."

"Is that it? You're torn with guilt and so delusional you'll blame the Game for your actions? Not that I don't, mind—they did provide you with a motive—but I'm not fool enough to eat your bullshit again. I knew you were phony when I saw the gun case. I only wish I'd been less gullible. Then Edgar might still be walking these streets where he belongs."

"I *loved* him," Reis sobbed. "I fucking loved him and now all the world thinks I'm his killer."

"That's because you are. There's video evidence. I had to see my godson murdered on television, Reis."

"The video is a fake! They used face-mapping technology. The Killing Committee—they want unrest between Kasyova and Anver. They want the Twin City-States to fall apart, and they don't care who they tread on to make it a reality."

"Do everyone a favor and get the fuck out of this country," Teon said. "You're not welcome here, and in all honesty, neither is Anver. We took you in when we had no obligation to. After years of mismanagement by corrupt governments and civil war, we came in and we fixed your broken-ass system. Now peace is in the toilet because of *you*."

"What can I do to prove to you I'm not the killer?" Reis pleaded.

"There ain't nothing you can do." Teon sighed. "Short of walking in with Edgar on your arm, alive and well, you're fucking dead to me. Don't think about bothering Leah, Ana, Kristy, or Sebastian either. Seb might even meet with you just to break your neck."

"I'm sorry," Reis said. "I shouldn't have bothered you." The call ended with a quiet click, leaving Reis alone in the broken greenhouse. They wiped their eyes, cursing their sentimentality. Now wasn't the time to feel. That ship had sailed when Edgar had been murdered. The only feeling worth holding onto was cold, hard vengeance.

They opened the gun case to check their sniper rifle. They took it apart and reassembled it, needing the busy work to distract from the gloomy thoughts running through their mind. Perhaps it would be better to kill themself. The world wouldn't miss them. Then they'd be with Edgar.

No. The Killing Committee wanted them dead. Reis was a loose end, the last person who knew their plan and cared to stop it. The best vengeance had to be justice, and they couldn't deliver it if they were dead. They still had one lead, the one they'd been chasing the night everything had fallen to pieces—Grady. If they found Grady, if they made him squeal, maybe they'd get something they could use. At the very least, they'd get to inflict pain on someone who'd made Edgar suffer so much.

They took out their handgun and reassembled that, too, counting their remaining ammo. They didn't have much, but they had enough to get the job done. It would only take one bullet in Grady's head to kill him. Or maybe they'd slit Grady's throat and nail him to a wall the way he'd done to Edgar.

Either way, Grady was going to pay. And then the rest of the Killing Committee would have to watch their backs—because Reis wasn't going to rest until each and every one of them was dead.

Chapter Thirteen

EDGAR

Edgar ached from lying still for so long. He'd tried to sleep, but he was fully rested and couldn't sleep any longer. The limited movement allowed by the handcuffs wasn't enough, and no matter how he writhed around, he couldn't find a comfortable position. He wanted to sit up, but bound as he was, it was impossible. All he could do was hope Grady came back soon—and he hated himself for that hope. He knew he was being trained for a torture from which there would be no end.

How he wanted to see Reis burst in through the door and come to his rescue. Reis had been his guardian angel, protecting him through it all, with no obligation to remain. Grady had been wrong—his feelings for Reis had nothing to do with Stockholm syndrome. He loved Reis's spirit, their sense of righteousness, their determination in the face of such impossible odds. Their brilliant light had given him hope when he'd been sure death was imminent. Now, Reis looked so desolate and broken, the footage from their arrest still playing on the television. Edgar wished he could reach out and touch Reis, let them know he was still alive and everything was going to be all right. He had to be content to sit and study the features of Reis's face, committing them to memory for the dark times that lay ahead. Grady would never let him go, but that didn't mean he had to submit in his heart or give up without a fight. So long as Reis's memory remained strong and bright, he could find a reason to go on.

It was late when the alarm buzzed, the lock clicked, and Grady let himself in. He looked tired. Edgar's first instinct was to rattle his cage, but there was no use baiting this unpredictable man. Perhaps it would be a better idea to play nice for now, so he wouldn't spend all night cuffed to this miserable bed.

"I've been thinking about what you said," Edgar muttered. "Nobody's coming for me, are they?"

"Nope. You're mine, now. The rest of the world thinks you're dead. Did you enjoy watching your own murder on television? How did it make you feel?"

It had been both odd and terrifying all at the same time, watching the grainy footage of Reis slitting his throat. It was so contrary to what he knew of Reis that it unsettled him to know it looked so convincing. If he hadn't known Reis better, he would have sworn to its authenticity as well. But the fact he was still here proved it to be a falsehood of the highest order.

"It was eerie," Edgar admitted. "Not every day you see someone killing your likeness. How did you pull it off?" Edgar asked. "Quite a feat to set up a murder scene like that and pin it on Reis. The likeness was uncanny. How did you make such a convincing prosthetic?"

"You assume it wasn't a real murder," Grady said. "That's where you're wrong. I knew I was only going to get one shot at it, and it had to look convincing. I couldn't risk a cheesy special effect giving the game away to the public. The Committee provided me with unlimited funds to get the job done and I made good use of them, let's put it that way. A real murder and a group of Dark Web deepfake enthusiasts more used to making celebrity porn than murder videos but happy to take my cash all the same."

"What a cop-out. Aren't you proud of your handiwork? Tell me the details—it's not like I'm going somewhere." Edgar didn't want to know, not really. It was disturbing enough to know it was all real, that someone, somewhere had died because of this sick game. Died in his place.

"It's not as interesting as you might think. I found a homeless guy who bore a passing resemblance to you, gave him a wig, paid him a million dollars in cash, and set him loose on the world. He wasted the money on hookers, coke, heroin, and alcohol, but I didn't give a fuck. He showed up at the address I gave him when he needed to and didn't ask a lot of questions. It was easy to get my Reis stand-in to slit his throat and nail him to the wall. Face-mapping took care of the video. Tricking the real Reis was a bit harder, but not by much. They were in so much shock they never really inspected your body. With what appeared to be your hair drooping over the corpse's face and so much blood obscuring everything, they never noticed the body wasn't yours. I made sure the cops hustled them off to the station before they could think too hard about it, and then I cleaned up the scene."

"I'm surprised they didn't kill you," Edgar said, trying hard to bury his disgust at what he'd heard. His stomach threatened to empty itself, but there was nothing left inside him to throw up.

"In front of so many witnesses, Reis wasn't stupid enough to commit a murder, especially when they were so confused."

"They'll be coming for you," Edgar warned.

"Of course." Grady scoffed. "Let them try. Reis was never anything more than an amateur with a gun who got lucky in the fact the people trying to kill you were even more unskilled than they were."

"I wouldn't call a group of armed mercenaries amateurs or unskilled," Edgar pointed out.

"Luck played a part as well." Grady shrugged. "I guess I should take off those handcuffs. You're looking a little stiff." He strode over to the bed and unlocked the cuffs.

Edgar considered taking a swing at Grady but knew it would harm him in the long run. If he was going to be staying here a while, it made sense to attempt compliance where he was able.

"May I stand?" Edgar asked.

"Go ahead," Grady said. "But try anything, and you'll be in a world of hurt."

"I know." Edgar stood and hobbled to the other side of the room; every motion painful yet a relief at the same time. He stretched out, glad to be a little more comfortable.

"How about you say 'thank you'?" Grady asked. He stroked the outline of his hard cock through his pants.

Edgar's mouth dried up in horror at the thought of having to service this man for the rest of his life.

"Not now. Bring me some food and water and maybe tomorrow." A plan was slowly forming in Edgar's mind. He wasn't going to be helpless and wait for Reis to rescue him. It was time he showed some backbone and took the fight to the Committee.

"Fine. Have it your way. One way or another you'll have to submit. One more day won't make much difference." Grady folded his arms. "You'll have food and water within the hour. Don't even think about escaping— this is a high security cell. I've got cameras and microphones trained on you, and the door is programmed to lock if the camera bot detects violence—so no, forget about punching the lackey I send with dinner."

Dinner. So, it was late. Edgar had been pretty sure of that from the tired bags around Grady's eyes, but now he was almost certain. Grady's shift was over, it was late, and he was tired. He was going to go home, have his own dinner, perhaps open a cold one, and go to bed. He wasn't going to stay at the Bureau and watch the cameras, he was going to let the bot do it.

Which was fine. His plan didn't involve violence, anyway. Reis was good at violence, but Edgar preferred to think through problems with logic and solve each one like a math equation. Judging from the tingle at the corner of his senses, he had almost stumbled upon a solution—if some of his assumptions turned out to be true, that is.

Grady left, and not a moment too soon. Edgar sat down on his bed, feigning tiredness in case Grady decided to stick around in his office for a while. The food and water arrived through a hatch in the door, and he ate and drank. He let an hour pass after that, knowing the next eight should be enough for what he needed.

Luckily, he'd avoided eyeballing the television remote control when Grady was in the room, and Grady had forgotten all about it. Televisions ran from the Internet these days, doubling as flat-panel computers to process the video data. The remote may not be advanced, but it was an input device he could use. It would suffice.

The other part of his plan involved Agent Vos. If she was as dirty as Grady was, he was shit out of luck, but he suspected she was the good cop to his bad one. All he needed to do was get a message to her requesting assistance at his location, and she'd have to come check it out. No agent would be able to ignore their curiosity on getting a message from a dead person. It couldn't be an essay, and he'd have to rely on some luck and hope she wouldn't go running to Grady with it, but it was as good of a plan as he was going to get.

As it turned out, it was easier than he thought. The television already came with a messaging app, and while they'd thought to lock out the Internet, they hadn't thought to lock out the internal network. Vos's username was already in the database, and it only took a few minutes to look her up. It took a few more minutes to painstakingly type a two-sentence message, and then he returned to the news channel to see Reis was still the flavor of the day.

It was in Vos's hands now, but hopefully by tomorrow the breaking news would be his return from the dead, and the clearing of Reis's name. He didn't know what he was going to do when he saw Reis, but he knew one thing: he wasn't going to waste any more time.

Chapter Fourteen

REIS

Reis breathed in as they sat in a rental car, scoping out Grady's home with a pair of binoculars. It had been easier than they'd thought to follow Grady home from the Bureau, keeping a car between them. Grady obviously didn't believe he was being followed, judging from the lack of care he took on his route home. Reis stopped and parked when they saw Grady disappear into a gated community. Scouting around the fence on foot, it didn't take them long to find a place where the fence was broken.

It seemed like they'd always been able to count on someone being careless or sloppy, but they weren't about to curse their good luck. It wouldn't have to hold much longer, anyway. Reis already knew, deep in their heart, that they didn't plan to live beyond taking down the Committee. It made the task at hand easier to bear if they didn't think about the legal ramifications of torturing and killing a Bureau agent and possible rebel sympathizers within the government itself. The police wouldn't care they were a traitor to their country, and they shouldn't. For the Twin City-States to survive, Reis had to put its future over their reputation as a citizen.

Whenever they lost their resolve, they thought of Edgar, slaughtered like an animal and nailed to a wall like a ritual sacrifice. All because of a political game he had no part in. The mental image still made Reis's gut churn, but they channeled their sorrow and grief into the more useful form of rage. Tears served no purpose here, but anger would see them get the job of serving vengeance and exposing the conspiracy done. If, somehow, they did manage to survive, there would be time for tears then. Time to mourn the one who'd died before—

No. Justice had to be served before they could let their mind stray. Every moment spent here was a risky one; they couldn't afford to lose the chance to strike while the element of surprise was still in their favor. Grady had no doubt expected Reis to run with their tail between their legs, to hide and plan and lick their wounds. In a week he'd be more on his guard, very much aware Reis might be coming for him.

Reis pressed their back against the wall of Grady's house. His car sat in the driveway, empty. There were no signs of family or other occupancy at the house, no second car or toys in the driveway, for which Reis was glad. They had no idea if Grady had a spouse or children, but the idea of exposing them to violence might have led Reis to rethink their plan.

Reis pressed themself up against the building and peered in through a side window. Grady sat with a beer and a TV dinner, watching the news coverage of Reis's release like he was seeing it for the first time. Reis thought about breaking the window and crashing in but decided against it. If the window didn't break easily, all they would be doing was giving Grady an opportunity to call the police.

Reis scouted around to the back of the house. They noticed an upstairs window wide open, and a porch roof that wouldn't be too hard to get onto. Grateful for their lithe body, they used the house's siding as a kind of scaffold and crawled onto the porch roof with only minimal noise. From there, it was child's play to climb through the window onto the upstairs landing. They tiptoed into the master bedroom, praying a creaky floorboard wouldn't give them away. They decided to hide behind the door and wait for Grady to come to bed, when he'd be at his most tired and vulnerable.

Reis had inherited their father's patience. As a sniper, Elias had often told stories of having to lie in wait for days, stalking a potential rebel target. Reis took their handgun from their waistband and held it close, ceasing all other movement.

The sun moved behind a dark cloud, and night came early as a storm moved in with a rumble of thunder and the sound of rain hitting the roof. Reis heard Grady throw his dinner plate into the sink and turn on the faucet. The low chatter of the television in the background fell completely silent as Grady killed the picture for the night. Reis's heart was in their mouth as Grady's weight made each stair creak on his ascent. They swore Grady would hear their shallow breaths or their heart pounding louder than a drum, but Grady didn't even give pause as he stumbled into his bedroom. He fumbled with the buttons on his shirt, slightly drunk as far as Reis could tell. His clothes landed in a pile at his feet. Grady threw his suit jacket and pistol belt over his chair.

He was never going to put it on again. Reis stepped out from behind the door and pointed the gun at Grady's naked back.

"Turn around slowly, hands on your head." Grady complied, resignation in his eyes as Reis stood before him. He eyed the gun on the chair, and Reis scoffed. "Make a move and I'll shoot you. Don't think I'm afraid to."

"Why are you here, Reis? What can you possibly stand to gain by killing me?"

"Vengeance. Justice for Edgar's death. But maybe we can make a deal if you hand over information on the Killing Committee. Who are they?"

Grady laughed, shaking his head. "Do you really think I fear you more than I fear them? I told you before they've penetrated the highest echelons of government. I'm just a lackey, a soldier, carrying out orders."

"Do you really believe Anver is better off without Kasyova?" Reis asked.

"Who can really say? Anver hasn't had the chance to self-govern since the failed military dictatorship. Nobody gave us a chance. Unification was paraded around as the best idea and the populace, so tired of war, would have eaten shit if it meant they didn't have to fight anymore. Perhaps it made sense at the time, but now look at us. Kasyova cares about itself first. Anver feeds off the scraps of their economy. Anverites contribute all our hard work, but it's Kasyova that takes all the credit." Grady shrugged. "I'm not a hardcore nationalist, not really. Just a man who followed others I admired into battle to pay off old debts. That's all. You're barking up the wrong tree if you think I'm going to drop their names."

"I don't expect you to sell them out without a little pain," Reis said. "Lay down on the floor."

"What are you going to do, Reis? Torture me? I'm a Bureau agent, and a soldier before that. I've been trained to resist torture. Besides, I doubt an amateur like you has the stomach for it. You should have stuck to petty revenge and shot me as soon as you walked in here." Grady laid down on the floor. "I didn't want to kill him, you know. I thought Edgar was quite attractive. Too bad he was smitten with your sorry ass. What a pair of fools, in over your heads. Well, at least you'll be united in death."

"Shut up!" Reis yelled, pressing the gun into Grady's temple while they held Grady's chest down on the ground with their knee. "You don't have the right to say his name!"

"You're pathetic, Reis. There's one thing I really don't understand about all this. Why did you decide to protect Edgar? At first, I thought it was because you knew more about the Killing Game than you were letting on, but it's become clear to me you have no clue at all. You're nothing more than a worthless bystander with an overblown sense of righteousness and absolutely no common sense."

"What do you mean?" Reis asked.

"Come on. You're the child of Elias Torell. I thought it was too great a coincidence to be chance, but apparently, I was wrong. You're a nobody. A shame, you might have proved useful..." Grady laid back and closed his eyes. As Reis looked on in horror, Grady started to seize violently. Foam bubbled from his mouth, and he fell still.

"What the fuck?" Reis shook Grady. "Wake up, you bastard! You don't get to take the easy way out! Not when you've cost me so much, damn it!" They beat their fists against Grady's chest, realizing this was the end of the line. They had no leads on the Committee, and the last hope of finding any information lay dead on the floor, suicide by cyanide pill. He'd known something, but his secrets had gone to the grave with him.

Edgar's death was avenged, but it was a pyrrhic victory at best. The trail was cold. There was nothing for Reis to do but to go back to everyday life and prepare for the coming war.

Chapter Fifteen

EMILY VOS

Agent Emily Vos rubbed her tired eyes as she stared at the monitor. She clicked in frustration to open the database window. Why did the damn thing insist on crashing so often? She'd have to put in a request with the help desk, which might take days before she could get any real work done on her workstation...

A window opened to a black screen: the command line prompt blinking. Perhaps the machine had a virus? It would explain the unusual behavior she'd been experiencing.

>*HELP*

Emily almost leaped out of her chair with fright as she read the message. Who was playing a trick on her? If it was that intern from IT again, she was going to file a formal harassment complaint.

>*BASEMENT*

>*CELL*

>*GRADY*

>*HELP*

The basement cells? Nobody had been down there in months. The high security cells were reserved for terrorists and prisoners deemed a threat to national security, neither of which were plentiful since Unification. If this was a joke to get her down there, she was going to be pissed. She closed the window. It had to be a joke, didn't it?

She continued searching the database when the window popped up again.

>*EDGAR*

>*TOBIAS*

>*IS*

>*ALIVE*

"What the fuck?" Emily whispered. This was getting way too creepy. She slid open her desk drawer, grabbed her gun, and holstered it around her waist. She felt safer with it there. She turned back to the screen, wondering if she should attempt a reply or whether she should go down to the basement and find out what was going on.

Deciding on the latter, she left her desk. Few agents had decided to stay late, so she walked to the elevator in silence. Scanning her keycard, she was able to select the basement level from the control panel and the elevator doors slid shut. She couldn't help feeling she was walking into some kind of trap, and hoped it was a surprise birthday party and not something more sinister. Grady had been acting strangely as of late, and she was starting to wonder if perhaps she was better off letting the whole investigation go. The Killing Game was over, after all. The Committee had either achieved their goal or gotten too spooked to continue. Edgar was dead, which was a shame, and the story of how Reis had come to betray him turned her stomach when she thought about it, but it was over. Nothing would change by digging deeper into it. Perhaps it was time to close the case file; her boss would certainly be all for it. She could get reassigned to Financial Crimes and start working with real people again instead of chasing after ghosts.

The elevator doors opened, and she stepped out. Most of the furniture down here was wrapped in shrink wrap, awaiting the day when a lone wolf terrorist decided Unification wasn't for them and tried to wage a war alone. Until then, the cells lay dormant, a reminder of Anver's violent past when the rebels had blown up civilians and the government had executed anyone who stepped out of line. Emily's father had surely come through these cells at some point... Emily shuddered, wondering how many people had spent their last days down here signing confessions under duress.

Unification had saved them from a dark era, and the Killing Game was a grim ode to it. That's why she'd practically crucified her career to work on the investigation. Anver couldn't be allowed to step back into a time of extrajudicial killings and politically motivated terror—and for what, some misguided sense of national and ethnic identity, as if Anverites were somehow genetically superior to their Kasyovan counterparts because their society had prioritized funding for the sciences instead of the arts?

Emily walked down the corridor, the soles of her boots creating echoing footsteps. Something about this place gave her chills and she wanted to leave as quickly as possible. She checked each cell, swiping her keycard against the electronic locks and finding sterile, empty rooms. Two more to check. One was empty. She braced herself for another empty room and a mystery unsolved as she scanned her keycard on the last door. What if this had all been some ploy to get her away from her desk? What if someone was deleting her files, ransacking her office? It had happened before. It would most likely happen again. Perhaps it was better she was out of the way.

The final door slid open. The lights were on. The television up in the corner of the room had the news channel running. She stepped into the doorway, suddenly afraid the door would slide shut forever and deny her the opportunity of seeing whoever was cooped up in here.

"I was worried you wouldn't come." Edgar Tobias sat on the bed, playing with the television remote control. He set it down. "We're not safe here. I'm sure you have a lot of questions, but we need to go now."

"Of course." Emily stilled her racing thoughts. Edgar was alive? Then... The entire story of Reis betraying him was a lie? To what ends? Who had taken the real Edgar and locked him up down here, where nobody would ever think to look?

Grady. It had to be Grady, and that meant he'd betrayed them, unless there was some really good reason why Edgar had cuff marks on his wrists. Edgar wasn't here for his own safety, that much was clear. No, this was a play for the Killing Committee, not against them. If Grady was compromised, that meant...

That meant everything Emily had discovered in the investigation up to now was compromised. The pieces fell into place, finally revealing the full picture. Of course, their enemy had always been one step ahead. They had a man on the inside, pretending to be as concerned about the rule of law as Emily. A man feeding her information, just enough tidbits to keep her chasing her tail while the Committee worked on their real goals.

At Edgar's urging, she dashed from the room. Edgar ran alongside her, and they reached the elevator. Emily looked at Edgar. "Where do we go from here?"

"I assume you've figured out Grady is dirty, and he was the one keeping me locked up in that hole, but Grady has his secrets too. The Killing Committee truly does believe I'm dead. Grady wanted to keep me as his own personal servant and sex slave, it seems."

"I don't suppose they cared what happened to you, as long as you disappeared. Their goal is complete. They've spun the narrative they wanted to tell—Anver and Kasyova are in chaos, believing the child of their beloved hero is nothing more than a treacherous killer."

"I need to find Reis." Edgar closed his eyes. "There's so much I have to tell them—and I need to stop them doing anything reckless in my name."

"Reis won't be easy to find. With a million dollars and not a care in the world, they can pretty much do whatever they want. Do you think they'll opt for vengeance right away?"

"Probably," Edgar admitted. "Reis thinks I'm dead—worse still, the whole world believes they're the culprit. Why wouldn't they be gunning for Grady? We were onto him. He'd been trying to blackmail me the whole time..."

"Seems like we go pay Grady a home visit. We need answers before he decides the game is up and goes underground." Emily tapped the button for the parking garage, tracing her fingers over the holstered gun at her side as if she might have to use it at any moment. Surely, they weren't going to let her out of the building with Edgar at her side? His discovery would be more than inconvenient for the Killing Committee, once it became known the entire killing was a sham.

"It might be wiser to go straight to the media," Edgar suggested. "Grady might decide it's better to kill us both. On his home turf, we're both at risk."

"Once the Committee know you're alive and well, they'll stop at nothing to see you dead. For your own safety, it might be easier to stay dead for a while."

"I have to clear Reis's name," Edgar said. "It must be tearing them apart, having the whole world believe they betrayed me. Besides, someone has to stop the riots. People are dying out there."

"I'm not sure they'll stop so easily. The pot has already been stirred... I wanted to believe the Twin City-States were perfect. Our lives have been a lot happier these past years than they ever were under the Anver state flag. But that's not true for everyone. A lot of jobs in science and tech have dwindled, leaving middle class families with no way to pay the mortgage and no hope for the future. That's not a genie we'll be able to shove back in the bottle simply by undermining the Killing Committee's story. Some will choose to believe exactly what they want to believe, no matter what conspiracy theories they have to come up with to justify it." Emily looked down at the carpet tiles in the elevator. "We've all turned a blind eye, Edgar, because we were doing okay. We didn't listen to the resentment that's grown and grown beneath the surface of our society. If that hatred never existed, the Killing Game would have been ignored. It was because Anverites had so much repressed anger against Kasyovans they were eager to participate in the game of killing their famous children."

"I've always loved Anver," Edgar admitted. "The individualist way of life here always made more sense to me than the community, arts-based society Kasyovans favor. But that's why we're stronger together. We make up for one another's flaws."

"Do we, though? It seems to me that other than a few people like you, most Kasyovans have stayed in Kasyova and most Anverites in Anver. The great melting pot envisioned by Elias Torell never came to pass. In the end, people like that which is familiar to them. Perhaps Unification is a social experiment that failed, and it's time to explore other options."

"You don't believe that. I'm sure you have a story about the civil war, like every other Anverite I've met."

"Yeah. My father was a rebel fighter in the civil war. He was tortured to death by the military government." Emily bit her lip. It still hurt to trace over those old scars. "He gave his life for the rebels to win, only for the weak rebel government to collapse in the end. I've often wondered what it was all for... Until now, the answer was peace. But if peace fails, what then? What was the purpose of his life...? Of his death?" The elevator door chimed, and Emily stepped out into the parking garage with Edgar in tow. "Maybe we're never meant to be happy. What if our purpose is defined by fighting for our lives?"

"That might be what the Committee believes, but I don't. We deserve peace and prosperity. Nobody ever said it was perfect, but we can work on it, instead of drawing divisions along racial and cultural lines."

"I hope it's not too late to save the Twin City-States," Emily said.

"Me too." Edgar climbed into the passenger seat of the black, shiny Bureau car Emily unlocked in the lot. She glanced furtively over at her personal vehicle, wondering if the brake lines had been cut or if the trunk was loaded with explosives. It wouldn't take much to kill them both and send the truth to the bottom of the ocean. They were more fragile now than ever. Perhaps Edgar was right, and he should run to the media, but deep down she knew if they took the safe bet, they would lose their chance to track down the real culprits while they were exposed.

Emily grabbed a Bureau hoodie from the backseat and threw it at Edgar. "Put this on and cover your face. Last thing we need is for you to be recognized." She calmly drove through traffic as he squeezed into the hooded garment, as if this were any other drive home after a long day's work. A summer storm rumbled overhead, and her wipers were on full, driving away the sheets of rain obscuring her vision. The gun felt heavy at her side. Would she really be able to use it on Grady if he threatened her? They'd been partners for so long, he felt like a brother. Even now, her mind was scrambling to find ways that might excuse his behavior, reasons why he could be a double agent. Some way to believe he was still honoring his oath to protect the Twin City-States.

She reached the gate that kept Grady's home closed off from the rest of the world. She knew the code, of course. She'd had to come here on many occasions to discuss work. Even as a friend. Being gay, he'd never made any leering advances or made her feel any less than completely comfortable in his presence. Her skin crawled now as she followed the implications of why he'd saved Edgar. To keep him as a slave. It was as if Grady had turned into a completely different person to the one she knew. How long had he kept this to himself, this treacherous, sinister person beneath the surface? Had anything about their professional friendship been real?

Emily pulled up on Grady's driveway. "Stay here," she said. "I'm going to leave the engine running. If you hear gunshots, get as far away from here as you can and go to the media." She walked up the gravel path and over to the front porch, where she knocked on the door. She hung about, trepidation and anxiety building in her gut as her knocks went unanswered. She tried the doorbell. More knocks. Nothing. The rain soaked her clothes and hair, intensifying her discomfort.

Something was wrong. Had Grady skipped town already? Not unless he'd left his car behind and taken a rental, at least. His vehicle still sat in the driveway, his Bureau parking pass hanging down from the mirror.

Emily tried the door. Locked. She kicked it in. Every instinct told her to stay outside and eventually it was the rain that forced her in. Everything was normal. She'd call out to Grady and he'd apologize for being in the shower or something. They'd sit down and have a talk and hash out why exactly Edgar had been in the basement. Maybe it had been for his own protection. Maybe. Hopefully.

"Grady?" Emily called out. She swore she heard a creak of weight shifting on the upstairs floorboards, but nobody answered her. A net curtain billowed from an open upstairs window on the landing. Surely, he would have closed the window rather than let the rain in? Emily drew her pistol and took the stairs one at a time, her back against the wall.

The door to the bedroom was open, and what she saw made her eyes widen and her mouth fall open as a flash of lightning illuminated the scene. Grady lay on the floor, his face ashen. No visible wounds or blood, but he was clearly dead. And there, sitting on the bed, looking lost, with tears streaking their cheeks, was Reis Asher.

Chapter Sixteen

REIS

Reis heard the car pull up. It was long past time to leave, but they'd been rooted to the spot by grief, fear, and anger. They sat down on the bed, losing the will to save themself.

Perhaps it was time to stop running and let themself be found. The trail was cold. The game was up. Edgar was dead. Grady was dead. Whatever happened next was out of their hands. If they went down for Grady's death, maybe that would feel like justice. They had intended to kill Grady, after all. They'd intended to pull out every toenail until Grady had pleaded for his life and spilled every tune he'd ever learned to sing.

That they'd not had the stomach for it didn't seem to matter. The fact that in the end, they'd had little to do with Grady's death didn't make Reis feel less like a killer. All the lives they'd taken in the course of trying to save Edgar seemed to rush in like water from a broken dam. The mercenary soldiers, going down one by one, blood and brain matter spreading across the stones in the greenhouse. So many people who would never go home to their families because Reis had gotten it in their head that they were some sort of guardian of the weak. A protector of Anver, and the peace their father had so carefully built and silently pledged to their care.

"You do what you have to do," Reis's father had once said. "If it's you or them, of course you'll choose you. That's human nature."

Yet all the killing had been for naught. Edgar had ended up dead after all, his throat slit like an animal. The scene haunted Reis's waking and sleeping hours, the image burned into their retinas like the shape of the sun after staring for too long. Reis doubted it would ever go away. Edgar would always live behind their eyelids, never the man he had been, only the corpse he had become. Grady had stolen everything from them—even Edgar's precious memory. Reis couldn't visualize his smile anymore, only the curve of the slit across his throat. His laugh was gone, replaced by the scream of pain and surprise from the video as he was brutally murdered.

The front door crashed open, hitting the wall with a loud bang. Vos's voice echoed upstairs. The house settled as the storm kicked up a strong gust of wind. Thunder rumbled. The stairs creaked as Vos came up, her senses leading her to this room. Would she shoot Reis when she found her partner dead at their feet? Reis half-hoped she would put them out of their misery. This living nightmare could finally end. They could find rest at last, regardless of whether they'd failed their purpose in life. They'd tried. It had to be enough.

A catch of breath as Vos saw the body. Vos raised her gun and Reis sat still, tears streaming down their cheeks. They'd done what they could to protect Edgar and Anver, and they'd failed. Vos would surely kill them or take them in, depending on what Grady had meant to her.

"Reis?" Vos asked, as if she wasn't sure it was really them in the low light. She leaned over and turned on the light. Perhaps sensing Reis wasn't a threat, she lowered her gun and knelt beside Grady, taking his pulse. Reis watched her go through the stages of grief one by one as she struggled to accept the scene before her.

"You didn't kill him." Vos's voice was quivering but audible enough for Reis to hear. "There are no visible wounds, no obvious head trauma... It looks like he choked on his own vomit."

"I think it was cyanide." Reis folded their hands in their lap. "Grady knew the game was up. I came here for information. I wasn't planning to leave without it. Now the trail is cold. The Killing Committee's plan is in action and I can't stop them. Edgar died for nothing. Everything I've done... It's all been for nothing."

"What if I told you Edgar was alive?" Vos's voice was quiet but firm. She stood from her crouching position beside Grady's body.

"I saw his body," Reis countered, fighting the sick hope surging inside their gut.

"Did you? Did you move his hair away from his face and really look, or did you take Grady and his sinister video at face value?"

"It would make no sense to keep him alive. He's a loose end. Finding out he's alive would undermine everything the Committee has fed the media." Reis fought the hope in their heart. Vos was speaking in hypotheticals, wasn't she? There was no way Edgar was alive.

"Emily?" A familiar voice echoed up from downstairs. "I know you told me not to come in, but..."

Reis's mouth fell open. They stood on shaking legs and rushed out of the room to the top of the staircase. They looked down the stairs and their eyes locked with Edgar's, his warm brown gaze struggling to penetrate the gloom.

"Edgar. Edgar!" Reis snapped on the light and rushed down the stairs two at a time, half stumbling, not caring if they fell. Edgar's eyes widened as he realized who was barreling toward him, and he opened his arms in time for Reis to skip the last couple of steps and dive right into them.

"Reis. Reis, you're safe." Edgar planted them on the ground and pulled them close. Fresh tears fell from Reis's eyes as they struggled to comprehend what was happening.

"But you... I saw you... They slit your throat..." Reis ran their hand along Edgar's face, the rough growth tickling their fingers as they caressed Edgar's chin and ran a line across their throat, the skin unblemished. Edgar was alive, and here in front of them. The knowledge took their breath away, and they had to suppress the urge to kiss him. This was not the time and place for tender feelings. Not with Grady's quickly cooling body upstairs.

"Not my throat," Edgar said, "but a person's throat, nonetheless. Grady engineered the scene to make it seem like I was dead. Instead, he took me to the basement cells at the Bureau. He claimed he wanted to keep me as a slave, but I doubt it was that clear-cut. I think he just... I think he couldn't bring himself to kill me. I think he *liked* me, though he had a strange way of showing it."

Reis gazed down at their feet, trying to look anywhere but Edgar's face, fearing judgement. "He's dead. I came here for information, and he bit down on a cyanide pill, and..."

"Hush. It's okay, Reis. I know why you came." Edgar kissed the top of Reis's head. If he knew the real reason Reis had come, of the murderous vengeance flowing through their veins, he didn't speak of it. "We have to get out of here. Go into hiding and hope we can strike from the shadows or go to the media and blow this thing wide open. I'll go along with whatever you decide."

Vos emerged from Grady's room and came down the stairs.

"Whatever we do, we have to make it fast. This is a murder scene—of a federal agent, no less—and you can't stay here. I'll do what I can to lead the investigation away from you, but you need to go into hiding while you decide what your next move is going to be. Do you have any ideas where to go?"

"Yeah, I have a plan," Edgar said. "Reis, I hope you're up for a trip to Kasyova. It's time to go and pay a visit to some old friends."

Chapter Seventeen

EDGAR

Edgar sat in Reis's rental car, watching the Anver-Kasyova highway speed by. Behind them, the tall concrete skyscrapers of Anver faded into the distance. In front of them, the outskirts of Kasyova started to grow up all around them. Brick-built homes with flowers and awnings welcomed them into the City of Culture as they passed by a sign that read "You have entered Kasyova." There was no sign of the barbed wire and the wall that had once stood tall at the border, keeping Anverite refugees fleeing its brutal civil war from pouring into its former neighbor.

Edgar remembered standing near the wall as a child on the other side, his fathers watching with sad, world-weary eyes as they waited to clear the checkpoint that would take them into Anver for a concert. They liked to play in Anver, despite having only a fraction of the popularity there compared to Kasyova. *"It's nice to play to a small crowd,"* Al had often said. Edgar had always looked up at Anver's huge skyscrapers. Even devastated by war, there was a mathematical symmetry to their construction that always fascinated him. He'd sat patiently in the bars his fathers affectionately referred to as "toilets" and watched them play a set, their speakers drowning out the air-raid sirens and the sound of gunfire outside. Demoralized, sometimes disfigured faces lit up with hope as they listened to the music, and Edgar knew, even then, this was the reason his fathers really came to Anver.

Now, he was returning to Kasyova after making a home in Anver. It felt alien to him, like slipping into another life he thought he'd left behind forever. Kasyova hadn't paused in his absence; the organic city growing and redeveloping so it was familiar yet foreign. There were new buildings on the skyline, dotted amongst the familiar golden domes of the Cathedral and the Silver Spires of the Galleria. The river still divided the cities like a scar down the middle, stitched over with a variety of bridges ranging from the ornate to the practical. Reis took the highway up onto the Central Bridge, where the best views of Kasyova could be found. They couldn't seem to help but look out of the window, even as they were driving.

"I've only been here a couple of times," Reis admitted. "It's not like I was invited when my father negotiated Unification."

"For someone who negotiated a merger of nations, you'd think your father would have been keen to imprint a sense of unity on you," Edgar replied.

"Not really. He's a nationalist and a patriot, really, strange though it might seem. He devised Unification because Anver literally had no other options after the rebel government collapsed. He was smart enough to know the power vacuum was likely to see Anver implode entirely or become swallowed by one of our larger neighbors to the East. It seemed like a favorable compromise to merge with a city-state the same size as our own." Reis focused on the traffic again as the busy highway demanded their attention. "This exit?"

"Yeah," Edgar said, retracing the route his fathers had driven so many times. "Keep left." Reis took the car under the bridge they'd just been driving over.

"The houses are so tightly packed, and all different shapes and sizes," Reis observed.

"They were built long before the advent of street planning." Edgar smiled. Most Anverites had difficulty with the narrow streets of Kasyova. He himself favored the open-plan approach Anver had taken, with lots of parks and greenery springing up since the war. Yet there was something comforting about the traditional brick row homes sprouting up on each side of them. There was a history in each brick Anver's new steel, concrete, and glass post-war reconstruction couldn't match. The trees lining the streets had stood there for generations, witnessing thousands of families playing beneath their branches in relative safety.

"Park by the side of the road, here," Edgar instructed. Reis pulled the car in, struggling with a sloppy parallel park before declaring it good enough and turning off the engine. Edgar got out of the vehicle and walked toward a house that had been converted from an old storefront. It made Reis think of their mother's florist shop.

"My mother was Kasyovan," Reis said. "She never returned after she married my father... The war made it too difficult. This place reminds me of her shop. I wonder if that was the intent?"

"Probably," Edgar said. "It can be hard to lose old habits. I wanted to come to Anver, but there were still things about Kasyova I missed. Despite being only an hour's drive, I never seemed to find the time to visit."

"We're here now." Reis stepped up to the front door and knocked. "Should we have called first?"

"Perhaps." Edgar stood in the doorway, trying to stay concealed from passersby. The wind blew, shaking the first fall leaves from the trees. The old wooden door creaked open, and Teon popped their head out.

"Who is—? Oh." Teon visibly paled as they set eyes on Reis. "Why would you come here? To rub salt in my wounds? You killed my godson. Why would you ever think you were welcome here?" Teon went to slam the door, but Edgar stepped forward and held it open.

"Because your godson isn't dead, Teon. Let us in. It's not exactly safe for me to be hanging about on the street right now." Edgar pushed past Teon's shocked face and into the house. Reis followed. Teon closed the door behind them, and the cozy gloom of the vestibule shrouded them in darkness. A mock oil lantern sat on the wall, the only light in the hallway. A thick rug covered hardwood flooring, and Edgar slipped his shoes off like he was home before separating the bead curtain that led into the living room. Incense burned in a corner, and nostalgia hit him like a wave, bringing many warm memories home to roost. Reis looked like they wanted to merge with the wall as Teon gave them a leery glance. Edgar placed a comforting hand on Reis's arm before pulling back his hood.

"I'm alive, Teon. It's really me. Reis didn't kill me. They saved my life," Edgar explained.

"Where have you been? I mourned you. I buried you in my heart, down deep, thinking you were with your fathers!" Teon started to sob. Edgar patted them on the shoulder.

"It's complicated," Edgar started and faltered as he considered how to give the most direct explanation without worrying Teon further. "I need to stay underground for now. The Killing Committee would not be happy to find out I am still alive. They may even restart the Game."

"Sit down." Teon ushered them into the living room, to a well-worn but comfortable couch. Edgar clasped Reis's hand without even thinking about it, leading them to sit instead of being frozen like a deer in the headlights. "You don't need to look quite so pale, Reis. You were right to bring him to me, and I thank you for keeping him safe."

"You believed I killed him." The hurt was obvious in Reis's voice, and Edgar was confused. What had transpired between these two in the hospital waiting room while he had hovered between life and death?

"With the news playing that video day and night, why would I believe otherwise? I didn't want to believe it, Reis, but the evidence was pretty convincing. I'm not going to lie—I've hated your guts pretty solidly for the past few days and there may be a few curses on your soul I'm going to have to undo, but let's face it, kid. The first time we met, you had a gun beside you the whole time. If it helps, I was disappointed when I heard the news. Disappointed and disgusted and heartbroken. I'm glad I was wrong about you. Gladder still to see Edgar walks the

Earth. It wasn't his time. Thank the gods." Teon wiped their eyes with their sleeve. "Tea?"

"Yes, please," Edgar said.

"If it's not too much trouble," Reis replied.

They sat in companionable silence as Teon left the room. Edgar liked the couch, especially the way it nestled him closer to Reis. It was hard to pull himself away, but he knew he needed to talk to Teon in the kitchen while they made tea. He squeezed Reis's hand before getting up and walking into the wood-paneled kitchen.

"Something's changed between you two," Teon pointed out.

"You don't sound too happy about that concept. Why? Reis protected me when they had no reason to. They put their life on the line for me over and over again."

"Exactly. Do you even know their motivations? Do you know anything about Reis, really? Do you know what their favorite food is, what they love to do in their spare time? Or are you developing feelings for them because they protected you?" Teon slammed the cupboard door and placed a can of tea leaves on the counter with more force than was necessary.

"Teon, why are you so angry about this? Do you think Reis isn't good enough for me? Or perhaps it's me. You don't think I'm good enough for them, do you?"

"That's got nothing to do with it. I simply don't want to see anyone get hurt." Teon's stance softened. "Soon, we're all going to have to pick a side, Edgar. Anver or Kasyova—not both, not with the way things are going. It's going to be hard enough for you with how torn you are, and you want to forge a relationship, now? With the child of perhaps the most famous Anverite of them all?"

"Their mother was Kasyovan, you know. Not that it matters. I made my choice long ago. You may keep hoping I'll change my mind, but I'm happy in Anver, with my freelance programming business—or at least I was, until the Killing Game began. I'd like to go back to it once this whole thing blows over."

"Their fame really bothers you, doesn't it?"

"Not as much as you think, Teon. I loved my fathers, and their music. Their passion for what they did was magical. But it's not my path. I wish you could see I'm equally as creative, in my own way—just with numbers instead of notes."

"You know, it never really bothered me," Teon confessed. "I missed you. I hated that you felt you had to move to Anver to pursue your dreams. Now, with the walls coming up once again, I worry I'll lose you forever."

"I'm sorry," Edgar said. "I've not been kind to you. I let too many years go by without keeping in touch. I don't know. It always seemed like you were disappointed in the path I chose. I felt your disapproval whenever we talked. It was easier to avoid you altogether."

"I'm sorry you felt that way, hon." Teon sighed. "I've not been the greatest godparent either. I promised your fathers I'd take care of you if anything ever happened to them, and I pushed you away instead." They let the tea steep and embraced Edgar in an awkward hug, which he returned with a smile.

"It's okay, Teon. As fucked up as it is to admit this, perhaps this whole experience has been a positive one. It's put a lot of things into sharp focus for me. Like how important people are in my life. I don't know what this is with Reis, yet, but I know it's important for me to explore this feeling. Maybe it will turn out to be nothing more than a deep friendship, but Reis is a hell of a person to have in my life, don't you think?"

"Remember, nobody's perfect," Teon warned. "You've seen the things they've wanted you to see—their courage, their determination—but everyone has flaws. Reis has done something tremendous in risking their life to protect yours, but don't let it blind you to the fact that in the end, they're a person like every other in the world. Don't hold them up to a standard that's impossible to meet, or you'll set yourselves up for disappointment and heartache."

"I know." Edgar glanced toward the door, wondering if their conversation was echoing into the living room. He didn't want Reis to think they were talking about them behind their back. There was more he wanted to say, but the thought of Reis and the knowledge he was still unpacking his own thoughts and feelings made Edgar move onto a different subject.

"Have you seen Leah, Seb, Ana, and Kristy lately?"

"Not as much as I'd like," Teon admitted. "Except Seb. He and I are dating. Don't give me that look. I know it's surprising, but at our age we're looking more for companionship than to set the world on fire."

Edgar nodded, a smile growing on his face. "I'm not judging you. I'm thinking about what my dads would say."

"They'd probably write a song about it." Teon grinned. "I kinda miss being the subject of their music."

"At least you didn't get to be their hit single. I think the whole of Kasyova still sees me as a tiny baby."

"Probably!" Teon put the teacups on a tray and led the way to the living room, the smile still set on their face. Reis sat patiently in the living room. They'd turned on the television. Talking heads talked about the future of Anver and Kasyova in the light of new tensions caused by the Killing Game.

"I hate watching this happen," Reis said. "I don't know if it would be better to come out and tell the truth, but the thought of putting your life in danger again..." They closed their hand into a fist, and Edgar sighed inwardly. He knew Reis was right, but the thought of plunging him and Reis back into the spotlight was anathema to every instinct he possessed.

"You're an excuse, you know that, right?" Teon piped up, setting the tea tray down. "The Killing Committee is only stoking tensions that already existed. They've accelerated the timeline with their actions, but the Anver-Kasyova partnership always had its fractures. Don't expect those to fade back into the night just because they know you're innocent and Edgar is alive. You're not as important as you think."

"I can't sit by and watch as my father's work is dismantled. He gave so much to protect Anver. I refuse to let it fall apart because of some manufactured *bullshit*." Reis buried their head in their hands, letting their chestnut hair fall forward like a curtain to cover their face.

"You're not the keeper of your father's legacy, Reis. Unification does not stand on your shoulders, but in the hands of the people. They are the ones who allowed it to happen, and if they decide it is over, there's nothing you can do to stop them." Teon held out Reis's teacup, waiting for them to be ready. Reis raised their head, taking the teacup in both hands with muttered thanks. "I don't want to see Unification end any more than you do. I may not completely understand or gel with the Anverite way of life, but the idea of watching our neighbor descend into civil war again is monstrous to anyone who lived through it."

Reis sighed. "There has to be a way to stop this trend. I refuse to be used like this—as a justification to begin a power struggle that can only end in war."

"For now, we have to sit tight," Edgar said. "I hate being the person to say it. It sounds like I only care about myself. Further interference on our part might cause more harm than good. Right now, people are angry, but their anger will settle down."

"Will it?" Reis closed their eyes. "I know Anverites. They're not going to stand there and let Kasyovans act like they're mortally offended at your death. It wounds their pride too much. They're going to rally behind the first demagogue who steps forward promising to restore Anver's pride and dignity." Reis sipped at their tea, seemingly lost in thought. Edgar paced, unsettled by the dark turn the conversation had taken. Couldn't they have some downtime, a break from the frantic pace of running for their lives, a moment to *breathe*?

"You can stay here for as long as you need," Teon offered. "I agree with Edgar on this one, Reis. I think we need to wait and see. Anything we do without knowing what we're stepping into risks turning a fracture into a full-on break. A few days won't make much of a difference either way, but it will allow you two to recover from the stress of being on the run."

Reis nodded, but their eyes lingered on the television screen as if they knew the future. Edgar excused himself to the bathroom. The tiny water closet felt like a womb, comforting and safe. He didn't have to run anymore. If Reis wanted to save the world, that was a conversation for another day. He flushed the toilet and looked in the mirror. Dark circles ringed his eyes, and he needed a good meal. Hopefully Teon's food would get him back on his feet before Reis felt the need to run off on their next quest. Despite acknowledging Teon was right in pointing out he didn't know anything about Reis, he was still sure he'd follow them to the ends of the world and back.

Chapter Eighteen

REIS

Reis started awake to find themself in a comfortable bed. They realized they were at Teon's house and stilled their hand before it could reach for the pistol sitting on the nightstand. Teon hadn't been crazy about Reis keeping loaded guns in the house, but Edgar had convinced them it might be necessary if things took a turn for the worse.

A turn for the worse. They both knew the tension between Anver and Kasyova wasn't simply going to dissipate as media interest in their story waned. The Killing Committee would make sure of that. The only reason they'd halted the Game was because they no longer needed it, which meant they had another weapon in their arsenal.

Reis hated waiting for the other shoe to drop.

They climbed out of bed and used the restroom before returning to the small attic bedroom they'd claimed for their own. It had formerly been used for instrument storage, judging by the number of black cases that sat around gathering dust. A piano stood against one eave, beckoning Reis to play a few notes. They relented with a bittersweet smile, recalling how their last link to their mother had been destroyed by the apartment fire Ash had set. What had happened to that bastard, anyway? After his botched attempt on Edgar's life, he'd disappeared like so much smoke. Was he just another player in the game, bribed to draw Reis in and dispense of them? It didn't matter. He didn't matter. If Reis saw him again, they were likely to land an uppercut to his jaw Ash wouldn't appreciate.

They hit a jarring, out of tune note on the piano and reveled in the discordance of it. It was hideous, out of place, wrong, like everything that had happened over the last month. They pressed more keys, creating a nightmarish tune in the early morning hours. They eased the lid down, realizing the noise was sure to wake the household. Teon and Edgar needed rest, even if Reis couldn't find solace and peace. Besides, the piano needed a professional tuner. It was an insult to music to play it this way, and their mother would have winced to hear it.

Their mother would have winced at a lot of things Reis had done, come to think of it. Reis wiped the dust off the piano with their T-shirt, analyzing the wood grain. Perhaps they should have gone into a career in music. Their mother would have smiled to know they'd followed their creative side, but there were far better musicians in both Anver and Kasyova. They'd continued to play almost out of loyalty to their mother, who had always loved to hear the classics played on a real instrument. Instead, it seemed their talents lay in pulling the trigger on a gun, just like their father. Fighting for peace. Was that an oxymoron? The sniper rifle sat in its case in the corner. Reis had brought it in from the car and moved the vehicle to another part of town before calling the rental company to come and pick it up. Having a car that could be traced to Reis Asher parked outside an associate of Edgar Tobias could only lead to inconvenient questions.

They knew they should leave. Edgar was safe here, in the company of family and friends. Nobody would chase after him now, and Reis was free to go after their political goals and stop the Committee by themself. Edgar wasn't really interested in getting involved, and that made sense. It wasn't his war, not really. He was an innocent bystander who had been used as a pawn in someone else's game, and Reis was reluctant to involve him further. But it was impossible to see Edgar's smile and broach the subject. They'd stepped around the topic for three days in the confines of Teon's house. It was nice to rest, but the clock was ticking. They couldn't stay, but...

But they didn't want to leave Edgar, knowing there was no real reason to ever come back. Knowing they might not be able to return if the forces at play were as powerful as they'd been led to believe. Did they really want to die having never explored the growing warmth between them and Edgar? The answer always came back as a resounding "no," and so they stayed, dancing around Edgar carefully as they kept one eye on the news broadcast. Reis's role in his life was unclear and grew hazier by the day. Edgar didn't need them, not really. If they didn't grasp the chance to explore their feelings soon, they might never do it.

A knock sounded on the door downstairs. Reis cleared their throat and declared "come in" as casually as they could manage. Edgar emerged from the small flight of narrow wooden stairs, a welcome sight.

Reis felt exposed in the borrowed T-shirt and pajama pants they were wearing. Their binder sat on the nightstand, underneath their pistol, and they folded their arms to try to hide their chest.

"I can come back if it's not a good time," Edgar suggested.

"No," Reis decided. "Or it'll never be a good time. Sorry if I woke you."

"Nah, I've been awake since dawn. I think I got enough sleep in Grady's cell to last a lifetime."

"What are we going to do?" Reis asked. It was useless to sit here exchanging pleasantries and small talk. Edgar had come for a reason, and it made sense to address the elephant in the room before it grew any bigger.

Edgar let out a long sigh. "Cutting to the chase, as always, I see. I suppose I should be grateful for that. I had a whole speech planned." He dragged over a nearby stool and dusted it off before sitting, putting him at an even level with Reis. "Teon said they're sick of the tension. I would have to agree."

"You know I can't stay," Reis said. "But I can't seem to bring myself to leave."

"We barely know each other. It would be stupid to jump into something that might not last."

"What does last, in this world? If two nations can't keep their union together, what hope do any of us have?" Reis buried their head in their hands.

"Even if Unification ends, we had a good ten years of peace. Anver was able to recover. Perhaps we could even hold a government together now."

"We? Do you still intend to return to Anver, even though it's likely to collapse on its own?"

"I didn't move there for the ambiance, Reis. I love the city. It's my home, now. I may have family here in Kasyova, but I laid my hat in Anver for a reason. I'm not about to abandon the city just because things are getting complicated."

"I have to fight for Unification. You know that, right? It's not about my father. I can't watch the city I grew up in descend into civil war again. I won't allow my friends to end up in the ground because of bullshit nationalism."

Edgar raised his eyebrows. "It might cost you your life to stand up for that belief."

"I know." Reis ran their hands through their hair, brushing it back over their head. "I know. I'm sorry. But this is what I was born to do. My purpose is to stop another civil war. If the world was kinder, I'd pursue other goals, but these are the chips I've been dealt."

"What would you do in that kind of world, Reis? What would a life of peace look like to you? Would you get yourself a new apartment and whittle away your years doing whatever it was you were doing before? Would you seriously take up the piano and try to make a living out of it? Would you join the military or become a cop or some other civic duty that called your name? Or would you find someone to settle down with?"

Reis smiled. "Why did I have to find someone to care about with the worst possible timing? It's a shame we don't have the kind of time I'd like. I overheard Teon in the kitchen, and they were right. We don't know anything about each other. But I'd like to learn about you, Edgar. I'd like to know what things you like. What your short- and long-term goals are. I'd like to know what you believe in and if you could ever fall in love with someone like me."

"I think I already know the answer to the last question," Edgar said. He pressed his hands together in his lap. "The real question is: are we too late?"

"I don't know," Reis lowered their eyes to the floor, tracing patterns in the floorboards. "I can't stay. No matter what happens between us."

"I understand." Edgar rose from his sitting position and closed the distance between them. Reis felt the air grow heavy between them, anticipation settling in like a dense fog. Edgar stood above them, every muscle in his arms seeming taut, holding back like an arrow on a bowstring. Reis stood to meet his lips, capturing them with their own. Edgar's eyes widened in surprise and Reis reveled in it, deepening the kiss until they were like two drowning souls. They parted for air, breaths heavy and rough.

"I have a question," Edgar whispered. "Why did you choose to save me?"

"Do you expect a noble reason, Edgar? A lofty ideal like the sake of the nation or the evil of murder? It was neither. You simply caught my eye in your stock photo." Reis scoffed. "I like to think I'm saving the world, but the truth is, I'm as petty and shallow as everyone else. I saw a guy I was attracted to and I thought it would be a damn shame if someone killed him."

"I think I like that reason better than some idealistic goal," Edgar whispered.

"Me too." Reis dived in for another kiss and let their hands roam over Edgar's ass. He wore tight jeans that left little to the imagination, and Reis could already feel his erection pressing up against their leg.

"What do you want?" Edgar asked. "I don't want to do anything you're uncomfortable with, but I'm starting to lose my mind here."

"One sec. Sorry." Reis darted over to the nightstand and grabbed their binder. They shucked their T-shirt with their back to Edgar and pulled the binder over their head. "There. Now you can do whatever you want. Don't panic, you won't get me pregnant. I opted to be voluntarily sterilized when I did my military service. Back then, they didn't offer top surgery or hormones, and I'm not sure I would have taken either if they had. Hell, I still don't know. I act like I have everything all figured out, but the truth is, I'm a big bag of uncertainty, Edgar. I battle with dysphoria on a daily, ever-changing basis. I hope you know what you're getting yourself into. You know, if you decide you want more than this."

"Did anyone ever tell you that you talk too much when you're nervous?" Edgar grabbed Reis's hand and placed it on the hard bulge in his pants. "Do you need any further evidence I'm attracted to you?"

"Mm, I'm not entirely convinced," Reis grinned. "Show me more." They unbuttoned Edgar's jeans and watched as he wiggled out of them, discarding his second skin on the floor. They raised their eyebrows at the fact he wore no underwear—had he come here seeking this encounter? Reis took his hard cock in hand, taking their time in deciding what they wanted. Perhaps this was it, this would be all—this one moment in the half-light before they parted forever—or maybe it was the beginning of something greater, the lighting of a torch that would keep on burning for a lifetime. "What do you like?" Reis whispered.

"I'm a simple man," Edgar replied. "There's not much I *don't* like, so surprise me." His eyes widened when Reis fell to their knees and ran their tongue along the underside of his cock, collecting a droplet of precum from the tip.

"I won't last if you keep that up," Edgar growled.

"It's a shame I lost all my toys in the fire," Reis whispered. "I'd love to fuck your ass into submission right about now." Edgar's cock twitched and Reis knew they'd hit a nerve. They took advantage, consuming Edgar's shaft with their mouth in one fell swoop. Edgar moaned and threw his head back as Reis worked his dick with their mouth, but it wasn't enough to scratch their itch. They wanted more. A joining of bodies. It had been a long time since they'd let anyone fuck them. They'd never given Ash the privilege, but then Ash had always made everything about him anyway. This was different. Edgar was different. There could be a lasting connection here—if they both survived the conspiracy. Or it could be one blissful encounter. Either way, Reis was sure they wouldn't regret it.

Reis let Edgar's cock slip from their mouth and stood up. They took Edgar's hand, led him to the narrow bed, and pressed him down on it. They wriggled out of their pajama pants and straddled Edgar's lap, grinding their slit against Edgar's dick until it was slick.

"You don't have to—" Edgar gasped, but Reis cut them off with a crushing kiss.

"Shh. I want to." Reis slid down onto Edgar's cock, impaling themself on it until Edgar was all the way inside them. Edgar groaned, throwing his head back as he bit his lip. Reis started to ride him, thrusting their hips to draw him deeper inside. It had been so long since they'd wanted anyone there, but Edgar had earned their trust. Edgar had placed his entire life in their hands, and it seemed like such a small thing to give some of that trust back, to allow Edgar access to a soft core they showed almost nobody. Something about the way Edgar always asked what made them comfortable made Reis feel safe showing a softer side in front of him—like he'd never doubt their gender identity because of it. There was nothing to prove to Edgar, and Reis felt like they could be themself without having to wonder what Edgar might be thinking.

Edgar reached up and stroked Reis's face, as if seeing them again for the first time. Reis smiled and upped their pace until the two of them were locked in a battle, panting and moaning together as the bed creaked and groaned beneath their combined weight. With a shout he muffled by biting his fist, Edgar came, spilling his seed inside Reis.

"I should have warned—"

"Shh. I wanted you to come inside me," Reis panted, still riding Edgar's cock. Biting their lip, Reis came, throwing their head back.

"Wow," Edgar whispered.

Reis climbed off Edgar and they lay down together on the bed. Reis felt uncertain now the moment had passed. Edgar's cum dribbled onto the bedsheets and Reis smiled, tracing lazy patterns and kisses across Edgar's smooth chest. Edgar wrapped his arm around them as Reis rested their head on his chest, listening to his heartbeat slowing back to a normal rate.

"I..." Reis wanted to say the words, but they stuck in their throat. It wasn't that they didn't mean them, but they represented a promise they might not be able to keep. If they went up against the Committee, what was the chance they'd come back alive? Telling Edgar they loved him was a cruelty by kindness, a request that he wait when they had no idea if they would ever be able to come back.

"I love you too," Edgar said, as if Reis had spoken their mind loud and clear. There was no hint of sarcasm in his voice.

Reis blinked back tears. "I wasn't going to..."

"Why?"

"Because they're going to kill me, Edgar. I know I have no chance of winning, and yet I have to go. I have to stop the Killing Committee."

"I know. That's why I'm going with you." Edgar rubbed a hand down Reis's back, soothing the muscles that had begun to spasm there, signaling their imminent retreat.

"You can't! I won't risk your life." Reis closed their eyes, wanting to avoid Edgar's earnest gaze.

"You're not risking anyone's life. It's my choice to go. I want to go. Anver is my country too. I want to defend it, same as you do."

A knock sounded at the door, breaching their little private world. Reis darted to their feet and rushed for their clothing. Edgar followed, fighting a war with his inside-out jeans leg that Reis would have found amusing if not for the gravitas of their conversation a second before. Reis answered the door like a chastised teenager caught with their prom date, knowing there was absolutely no way Teon couldn't know Edgar was in here with them.

"I'm sorry to interrupt," Teon said, the look in their eyes one of absolute seriousness. "I think you both need to see the news. There's been a terrorist attack."

Chapter Nineteen

EDGAR

Edgar's heart pounded in his throat like it might suffocate him. "Where?" As if it mattered where. As if Anver was a better place to blow up than Kasyova, or vice versa. People were dead, and judging from the horrified look on Teon's face, it was nothing short of a massacre.

Edgar turned around and saw the color had drained from Reis's face. Tears in their eyes, they pushed past Edgar and Teon and went into the living room. Edgar followed, Teon trailing in his wake. Incense still burned in the corner of the cramped living room, and the enormous flat-panel television seemed to take up most of the front wall, broadcasting images of bodies strewn about like broken dolls. The Galleria, home to some of the rarest art pieces in the world, burned, smoke coiling upwards into the sky as priceless human lives burned along with their masterpieces.

"The bomb went off at eight a.m., as the gallery opened. It seems to have exploded in the vestibule area, where crowds awaited the opening of a new exhibition dedicated to Anverite art... Hold on, we have breaking news. A video is being streamed on the Killing Game website. We're going live now..."

A figure appeared on screen, a familiar face standing stoic in a suit and tie. The Anverite rebel flag hung behind him and a sinking feeling settled in Edgar's gut.

"That's Tony Anvas... I guess he's not hiding his rebel connections anymore... Or his connection to the Committee." Reis shook their head. "If I'd had evidence, maybe I'd have been able to go after him, but a man that powerful practically owns the media..."

Edgar placed his hand on Reis's shoulder and squeezed. "It's not your fault, Reis."

Tony Anvas cleared his throat. "Today we take back what is ours. Today we declare war on the failed policy of Unification, which has seen Kasyova prosper while we feed off its crumbs! This art exhibition is only one example of Kasyovan subjugation. They've only ever been interested in what Anver can provide for the arts. Technology and medicine, Anver's strengths, have been thrown to the dogs so Kasyova can force its agenda on us. No more! We may have been weak when the tanks rolled in, but now we are strong enough to take back Anver for Anverites and forge a government with Anver's interests at its core. The new rebel movement is born this day in blood, with a promise to Kasyova that your streets will run red with it unless you give our city-state its independence!"

"Bullshit!" Reis yelled. "If you cared about Anverites, you wouldn't have killed all those who lined up at the gallery to show pride in their own people's art!"

"He can't hear you, Reis. A monster like him wouldn't hear you if you stood right in front of him. Save your strength." Edgar pulled Reis into his embrace from behind, offering his support. He half-wondered if Reis would shrug him off in anger, but they seemed to allow and even welcome the comfort.

The broadcast switched back to the anchor, who looked visibly shaken. "We're waiting on a statement from the Twin City-States President, who has called a meeting of the Emergency Cabinet to discuss their options. In the meantime, we advise everyone to stay in their homes. Police are searching for a suspect shown in these images taken from video cameras at the gallery, which seem to depict a man placing packages in two nearby trash cans... The suspect is still at large and is considered armed and dangerous." An image popped up on screen. Edgar was sure he'd seen the man somewhere before but couldn't quite place him. Reis seemed to pale even further and looked like they might collapse. Edgar held them up as they crumpled in his arms.

"It's Ash. My ex, the one who burned down my apartment. The one who told me about the Killing Game in the first place. I can't believe he's been working with the Committee all this time..." Reis slipped out of Edgar's arms and stumbled to the couch, where they slumped down into it. "I can't... I can't believe this... This has to be a nightmare!"

"Reis." Edgar placed his hands on Reis's shoulders. "Focus. Lives may depend on it. Do you know where he might have gone?"

"I don't know... Ash doesn't have many friends. He used to like to crash at my apartment, even after we broke up. Said he had nowhere else to go, and I was the sucker who believed him."

"Your apartment is nothing but a burned-up shell, now. Do you think he might still go there?"

"I have to find out." Reis swallowed. "If he did this... I have to take him down." Reis stood, resolve in their eyes. They marched upstairs. Edgar stood, watching the television, feeling helplessness wash over him. He knew it was no good trying to talk Reis out of it. This had become more personal than ever. Reis would never let it go.

"Aren't you going to do something?" Teon asked. "You're not planning on letting Reis walk out of here with two guns and a score to settle, I hope?"

"No. I'm going to go with them and hopefully stop them doing something they'll regret. Can I borrow your car, Teon?"

"I should tell you no. Taking on an armed terrorist— you have gone off the deep end. Yet it's the most passionate I've seen you about anything. Like you might write a song about it if that was your jam." Teon grabbed their keys from a hook and tossed them to Edgar. "Do what you have to do. I'm proud of the man you've become."

"Thanks," Edgar said. Reis bolted down the stairs and out of the front door. Edgar followed them out onto the street.

"You'll need transport, Reis. I'll drive. Think up a game plan on the way." Seeing Reis give him a look of refusal, Edgar shook his head. "I'm coming whether you like it or not, and you don't have a choice, seeing as I have the car keys."

"It's my job to take down Ash. I was the one who kicked him out, leaving him homeless. Is it any wonder he found a cause to latch onto?"

"I don't know what your situation was, but I refuse to believe it was that simple." Edgar opened the car door and climbed in while Reis put their sniper rifle case on the backseat and jumped into the front passenger seat.

"Let's go. I don't know how long he'll hang around." Reis disassembled and reassembled their pistol while Edgar drove. Edgar caught a glimpse of the five bullets left in the magazine, but they didn't have time to stop for ammunition. He tried to think of the layout of the apartment, despite having spent so little time there. Reis was in no mood to come up with a sensible game plan. Edgar could stay more detached since it was less personal for him.

"You have ammo for that rifle?" Edgar asked.

"Yeah," Reis said.

"There's an abandoned apartment complex across the street from your place, right? I remember seeing something like that."

"Yeah. It was damaged back in the war and condemned, but it was never knocked down."

"I'm going to assume you want to confront Ash. Let me cover you from over there." Edgar eyed the rifle in the back seat with baleful eyes. He didn't want to shoot a man, but if Reis went in alone and gave pause because of Ash being their ex, it could be a fatal mistake. They hadn't come this far only to die here.

"You're not a soldier. Could you pull the trigger and take a life if it comes down to it?" Reis's eyes widened in surprise.

"I completed the same mandatory military service you did, Reis. Just because I hesitated at the florist doesn't mean I'll make the same mistake twice. Ash has murdered civilians, and he'll strike again if he's not taken down. Trust me. I want to believe we can take him into custody, but you and I both know he's probably resigned himself to dying for a cause."

"We were both so purposeless..." Reis mused. "We were on a long road, going nowhere... And we took it out on each other. He liked to gamble. Got himself in trouble. But I wasn't any better. I liked to tell myself he abused me, but we tormented each other. What we had wasn't healthy, Edgar. I liked to goad him into hitting me. I used to say the worst things to get a rise out of him. Now he's found his purpose. I can't help but think I pushed him down the path he's on."

"He wants you to believe that. He'll use it against you. Reis, you're not responsible for his choices. You didn't put a bomb in his hand and tell him to murder those people. You didn't hand him a gun and tell him to come after me either. Regardless of your history, you're going to have to accept he's not the guy you loved."

Reis nodded. "That may be true, but I have to try to take him in."

"Of course. I'd be concerned if you wanted to kill him outright." Edgar reached over and placed his hand on Reis's leg. Reis placed their hand over his as they pulled up at the end of the street. "We should probably go on foot from here."

Reis reached into their backpack and handed Edgar the cellphone the Bureau had given him before checking their own was present and charged. "Text me when you're in position. Let me know if you have any problems."

Edgar got out of the car and shut the door. He took the sniper rifle case from the back seat. "Good luck, Reis. I'll see you on the other side."

"Right." Reis inhaled a deep breath and slowly exhaled. Keeping their pistol low, they pressed themself against the building, staying out of sight from anyone looking down from above. Edgar crossed the street, hoping this wasn't the last time he'd see Reis alive.

Chapter Twenty

EDGAR

Edgar darted down a back alley. The shell of the old office building opposite Reis's apartment block loomed over everything, a giant bomb crater sitting next to it as a stark reminder Anver had been embroiled in civil war only ten short years ago. The windows had shattered, leaving the skeletal framework as a grim testament to the horrors that had engulfed this city.

To think they'd come so close to the brink of war again. What the Killing Committee had done was unforgivable, stoking tensions into a frenzy like this. He thought of the bodies at the art gallery, people who wouldn't be going home today because they'd wanted nothing more than to enjoy a mesh of Kasyovan and Anverite culture. To hell with the idea of national identity when it became a wedge to drive people apart. He may have never felt truly at home in Kasyova, but the songs of his fathers had only enriched the world, giving more to it. He would defend the Twin City-States from those who wanted to take that joy away or punish people for indulging in it.

Edgar stepped over the threshold, through a back door that had been blown off its hinges. The building was dark, but the daylight gave him enough light to find a path through the abandoned interior. Ceiling tiles hung down, damp and moldy. Metal lockers rusted, their doors pried open by looters looking for anything they could use. Decayed pieces of paper and broken glass covered the floor. Edgar stepped over it all, heading to the stairwell. Graffiti lined the walls, tags from various groups past and present. The stench of urine was strong as Edgar climbed. He wondered if he would find homeless people using the windowless stairwell for shelter, but the building seemed thankfully deserted.

Every few floors, Edgar would go to the other side of the building and see how far up he was. Reis's apartment stood out like a sore thumb on the other side of the street, the scorch marks on the siding cutting across the building like a scar. It had been contained quickly from the looks of it, for which Edgar was grateful. He remembered the families running for their lives and hoped most of them had been able to salvage their things, at the very least. It seemed like years since the Killing Game had started, knocking him out of the safe, isolated life he'd been living. He felt like a different man to the one who had been content to lock himself in his apartment for most of the day dealing with clients. The world had seen fit to remind him it still existed and he was a part of it, even if it had been a rude awakening.

At least it had brought him Reis. Between the terrifying moments of knowing he probably wouldn't live to see out the year, Reis had always been there, protecting him. They could have left at any time, but they'd stayed. If the two of them got over this final hurdle, perhaps they'd have a chance at some kind of ordinary life. What kind of life would Reis settle for, in a normal world? Come to think of it, what had they been doing before the Killing Game? Not a lot of anything, it seemed. Perhaps they had a new lease of life now—Edgar knew he did. Even though he hadn't lost his passion for coding and planned to go back to freelancing, the world seemed different, now. The sunlight was a little brighter, the colors a little more vivid. Things seemed to matter more.

Would Reis even want him once they were done here? Could they turn their feelings into something long-lasting, or was it destined to be a fling that had culminated in their tryst back at Teon's house? He hoped not. Something about Reis drew him in, layers peeling back to reveal deeper, even more interesting aspects of their personality. Edgar wondered what kind of life would make Reis satisfied. Maybe they'd sign up for the military, to defend the Twin City-States? Or perhaps they'd want to serve their country on a more local level, as a cop, or maybe a politician. Nah, he couldn't imagine Reis the politician. They were too honest for that. The Bureau, maybe? Now that seemed like a good fit—if they qualified.

If they made it that far. There was no guarantee that Ash was actually here, after all. It was nothing more than guesswork on Reis's part, though their instincts were usually good. What better place to hide than a condemned, burnt-out apartment where nobody would think to go?

Edgar kept low and shuffled across the remains of the office. Looking out of the window frame, he knelt and unclasped the rifle case. He assembled the rifle clumsily, recalling his military drills. He drew the sniper rifle up and peered through the scope. He could see into Reis's apartment, all right. Singed wallpaper peeled from the walls. It was a total loss, Edgar realized, with a pang in his gut. Reis had given everything up to save him. To protect him. He was only drawing breath now because Reis had chosen to shield him. He didn't feel worthy of the honor but was grateful regardless.

He eyed a figure pacing around in the apartment. Ash. He brought the sniper rifle back and loaded it, ensuring everything was ready to go. He texted Reis and waited for confirmation. He watched through the scope as Reis entered the building and disappeared from view. Looking through the window in the stairwell, he saw Reis creeping upwards with measured footsteps, keeping silent like a professional. They hadn't taught that in the military. Reis had clearly picked up some tricks as a child of war, their life shaped by living in a city under siege by its own people, divided up like a pie between factions. They'd become a soldier without realizing it, a child born to fight, and yet they hadn't lost sight of their ideals. Reis was a true warrior, living by a code of their own.

Reis reached the same floor as Ash. Edgar moved the sight back over Ash, who seemed oblivious to the fact Reis stood against the wall right outside the apartment. Ash circled the apartment like a caged lion, alternating between chewing his nails and checking his gun. Edgar thought about texting Reis to tell them Ash was armed but was afraid of making a sound—and besides, Reis wasn't dumb. They knew Ash would have to be armed. Better to stay trained on Ash and try to still his own shaking hands. There was no way he could take the shot like this and hit, but he couldn't help it. He'd never killed before. He'd grown up in Kasyova, and the only war he'd seen was as a tourist with his fathers. It had always seemed distant, their manager spiriting them away before anything could get too violent or risky. Their military training had seemed like a college class, teaching the theory of how to kill without having to pull the trigger on a real human being.

This wasn't training. When he pulled the trigger, a human being would die. Reis had managed it in the greenhouse, taking down soldiers left, right, and center. Edgar had hesitated and gotten a bullet to the gut for his trouble. This time, though, it wasn't his life on the line, but Reis's. If he missed, if he held back, it was Reis who would pay the price.

He couldn't afford to hold back. He'd only get one shot before Ash was aware of the sniper, and the chance of him hitting a moving target was next to none. Panic started to spread through Edgar's veins, a little voice in his head doubting he'd ever be able to pull the trigger. Maybe, he hoped, it wouldn't come to that. Reis might yet be able to talk Ash down.

As the door opened and Reis and Ash pointed guns at each other simultaneously, Edgar realized that wasn't going to be a possibility.

*

REIS

"Reis. I'm glad you came." Ash stood in the blackened living room, looking much thinner than the Ash Reis remembered. Dark rings circled his bloodshot eyes, and the white dye he'd always loved to color his hair with was growing out, revealing the black roots underneath. He held his pistol up, and Reis responded in kind.

"Why did you kill those people?" Reis asked. "I never figured you to be a killer."

"Maybe I thought it would bring me closer to you." Ash looked Reis in the eyes. "You have your father's eyes. Soldier's eyes."

"I never wanted to be a killer," Reis said. "I did what I had to do and nothing more."

"Don't lie. You never were any good at it. The Killing Game gave you what you really craved. Something to fight for, something to protect. A cause. A reason to kill. A purpose in life. Isn't that right?"

"Last I checked, I didn't blow up innocent civilians. I only killed those who threatened Edgar. Even then, I hesitated. I should have killed you when I had the chance. Now tell me why. Why did you join the Killing Committee? Why are you working to destabilize Unification?"

"Do you remember how I loved the adrenaline rush of a big win at the casino, Reis? It felt like a purpose. I didn't even care about the money. I loved to win. I'd take home a big haul and I'd be so high on the rush we'd fuck all night. Remember that? Well, I've found a bigger rush. A higher purpose. I know what you see, now, Reis, when you play with your guns. I didn't get to experience the war like you did. My father had so much money he insulated me from the worst of it. He didn't come home with blood-stained hands or give me knowledge on how to fight. I had to learn it for myself. I see it, now. We all need a reason to live... What if that reason is simply the struggle to survive?"

"What are you talking about?" Reis asked.

"You know what I'm talking about. Anver's independence. It won't come about without a war with Kasyova, and I've fired the first shot across their bow. The ripples of what I've done will shake Kasyova like an earthquake. For the first time in my life, I've made a change in the timeline. I'm shaping the history books."

"You've torn people from their families! You don't have the right."

"You gonna get all high and mighty on your pedestal up there, Reis? Yeah, I guess you would. You've always liked to cover the animal you are with a veneer of civilization. You'd sit at the piano and play, but truth is, you wanted to fight. That's why you'd always pick battles with me. You loved to tussle and fuck. Those were the only times you ever felt alive. It's not your fault, Reis. You grew up knowing nothing except fear. Your body needs it, now. It craves adrenaline like a drug. That's the only reason you chose to protect *him*—to liven up your boring, hopeless life. I played you like a fiddle, and you couldn't help yourself. But you killed him in the end. Your killer instinct won out."

"Shut up!" Reis yelled. So, Ash still believed Edgar was dead. That was good to hear, at least.

"You only hate hearing the truth. It's okay. The truth can be hard to hear. I had to get used to it as well. When the Committee approached me, I was horrified. I wanted nothing to do with Anver's independence or murdering civilians. But they knew what I needed. They knew what I'd seen in you. They knew I was craving a reason to go on... They gave it to me. You can have it, too, Reis." Ash reached out his hand. "Join us, and you'll never have a boring life. We'll take Anver back together. We'll kill anyone who stands in our way, and we'll go down in history as the ones who ripped Anver away from its overbearing parent, Kasyova. We'll wash our hands in blood, knowing we love the fight more than the outcome—we're soldiers, born to kill."

"You're forgetting something important," Reis said. "Nobody wants a war with Kasyova. Me least of all. I lost my mother in an air raid. She died in front of me as our house crumbled on top of her. I wouldn't wish that nightmare on anyone. I spent every day afraid I'd lose everyone I cared about—and I did. I lost both my parents to the war."

"Don't be melodramatic. Your father's still alive."

"Dad drools into his dinner. In his lucid moments, he tells glory tales of the war he single-handedly ended. He was a hero to the nation, but it deprived him of the ability to be a father to me. Everything he taught me was about how to fight and survive. Every lesson he gave was designed for a soldier, not a child. Except I grew up in a land that was finally embracing peace. I never learned how to live a normal life, Ash. I never had the chance to know what the purpose of a life without fear and adrenaline was."

"It's boring, Reis. Pointless. I was a nobody. No matter how hard I worked, I would always be a nobody. Nobody would ever know or care that I lived."

"That's not true. I cared."

"You cared about pretending to be normal. About suppressing your true feelings. Trying to squeeze us both into a nine-to-five schedule like we could be ordinary. It mattered so much to you, but it was killing you inside. You never lied to the world about your gender identity, so why did you feel the need to lie about your thirst for the fight? Even now, after you slit Edgar's throat like a pig, you're still trying to hide it."

"Because I don't want to kill, Ash. I don't enjoy it, and I never want to enjoy it. That's why I never joined the military once my mandatory time was up—because I was afraid I might like it too much, that killing might become as normal to me as it became to my father."

"Yet you're standing there with a gun in your hand, a murderer who walked away with the prize. You can't tell me you don't intend to use it. You know me well enough to understand I won't submit and be hauled away to rot in a jail cell. I'd rather die at the top of my game."

Reis lowered their gun. "I don't intend to use it. I can't shoot you. I did you wrong. I made this monster you are today."

"Then you'll die, Reis, though I'm hesitant to shoot you down in cold blood. I was hoping for a fight like the old days. A fight to the death like the killer you are. Something to stir my blood."

"I'm sorry to disappoint," Reis said, "but I'm not the person you think I am. I'm not a warrior. I'm a protector, and the Twin City-States—and all their citizens—are my charges. I don't love killing. I love preserving this peace so many gave their lives for. I love keeping my father's legacy safe, so people can live their lives without fear."

"How can you moralize like that after slaughtering a man who trusted you in cold blood? How deluded are you, Reis?"

Reis raised their pistol. It was kill or be killed once again, but their hands shook. Ash wasn't a faceless, masked mercenary. As fucked up as their relationship had been, they'd shared every intimacy possible. They'd operated on a level of trust few ever experienced, bound together by passion and fury and fire hotter than a thousand suns.

But they'd burned up, leaving only ashes. Reis didn't want that life anymore. They liked the gentle kindness and stability Edgar offered. They'd started to imagine a life where they could sit at home and watch Edgar write code on the couch. Of lazy Sunday mornings where they'd get up slowly and enjoy the peace they'd taken for granted up until now.

"Do it, Reis. Kill me and embrace your true nature. Kill me like you killed him. Carve me up and nail me to the wall. Do it. You know it's what you want."

"No," Reis said. "It's what *you* want." They lowered the gun. Ash raised his pistol, and Reis stared down the barrel, knowing they'd made a fatal mistake. It was kill or be killed, and they'd given up the chance to kill, leaving only one option: death.

*

EDGAR

Edgar watched the scene play out, wondering what was taking so long. From their body language, he could tell Reis and Ash were arguing, raising and lowering their pistols as they did so. Edgar's tension only built, the tremor in his hands intensifying as the drama stretched onward.

He knew, deep in his heart, Ash wasn't going to turn himself in. Nor was Reis going to shoot him, judging from the uncertainty on their face. Ash had to know Reis wasn't going to pull the trigger. He was toying with them now. Edgar thought about taking the shot, but if he didn't give Reis time to negotiate, Reis would never get the closure they needed. He had to be patient, but patience was killing him slowly. His chest ached from the pounding of his heart. He felt breathless from the shallow, unfulfilling gasps he took, never really sating his lungs. It had to end soon, one way or another. He was done, his body and mind strung out, finally reaching its limit after months of uncertainty and fear.

How had Reis survived an entire childhood this way? How had they managed to dodge death every single day and not fall apart? It was exhausting to live like this, a half-life spent wondering if each moment would be his last. Edgar wanted it to be over, even if it ended in his death. It had to be less frightening than always living in fear of losing everything he loved. He couldn't handle it anymore. He was unraveling like a spool of thread. His fathers had raised him for a life of peace and love. His mandatory military service had seemed like a ridiculous hurdle and he'd hated it, often passing the time by calculating angles and trajectories. Perhaps, if he did that now, he could take the shot and be done.

He returned his focus to the scene. Reis lowered their gun, seemingly defeated, and Ash wasted no time in raising his gun to Reis's head. He pressed the barrel against Reis's temple, daring them to fight back, but Reis stared him down, looking him in the eye as they made their last stand. Edgar knew that stubborn look—he'd been on the receiving end of it a few times now. They'd die, but Reis would never surrender or submit.

Edgar took the shot without stopping to think of time or trajectory. The final moment had come, and it was kill or be killed—the law of the jungle. The law of the world people like Ash occupied, a world of bloodshed and chaos, standing contrary to the rule of order and law Reis loved. That was the difference between a soldier and a killer. A soldier obeyed rules. A killer followed instincts.

Which was he? Edgar wondered, as the bullet left the barrel of the gun. It seemed to travel forever in slow motion, crossing the space between the two buildings. He readied himself for another shot in case the first one missed, but he saw a spatter of red through the scope and knew he'd hit the mark.

Ash crumpled to the ground. Reis rushed to his side. Edgar thrust the gun down, suddenly disgusted with it and the circumstances that had led to this. His stomach churned, and he vomited on the ground, tears mixing with the contents of his stomach as his body fought between sobbing and puking.

He was a killer, now. He'd killed Ash to save Reis, but the knowledge offered him little comfort. Nor did the fact that Ash was a terrorist who'd killed civilians in cold blood. There was no justification for murder. Had Reis felt this way protecting him in the greenhouse when they'd killed a dozen mercenaries to save him? Had they suffered all this time in silence, standing by his side, saying nothing?

Edgar packed the rifle in the case and picked it up. Reis needed him now. What was done was done and could not be undone by any mortal means. All he could do was go to Reis and comfort them.

*

REIS

Reis stared Ash down, mentally daring him to pull the trigger. They would not beg or whimper for their life. If Ash killed them here, so be it. They'd found their purpose in life—to protect their country and all the people in it. Edgar would survive. He'd be able to contact Agent Vos and they could use the distraction of Reis's death to take Ash in.

A shot rang out. Ash's chest exploded in a mess of blood and guts. He crumpled, falling in on himself, his broken body shattering further as he landed on the scorched carpet.

"Ash!" Reis darted to his side, kneeling over his body. They didn't have to see the stain of blood pooling on his shirt to know he wasn't going to make it.

"Who?" Ash reached up. "Who shot me?"

"Edgar shot you." Reis closed their eyes. "I didn't murder him, Ash. The video was a setup made by Grady to make it seem like I did."

"You protected him? He's alive?" Ash looked up in confusion. "You beat the Killing Game. Heh. I thought you were your father's child. A natural-born killer. I guess I was wrong after all."

"What do you mean?" Reis asked.

"You should ask him yourself." Ash slumped in Reis's arms, the light in his eyes flickering out like a candle deprived of oxygen. Reis set his body down and closed his eyes. They stood on shaking legs, trying to fight the rush of feelings that swam through their mind. There was no sense in grieving for Ash. He'd chased death's shadow until he'd become engulfed by it. His chaos had eventually consumed itself.

Edgar had actually made the shot. He had to be a wreck. Reis wanted to go to him, but there were other matters to attend to first. They wiped away the stray tear leaking from their right eye and pulled out their phone to call Vos.

"Agent Vos," she answered. "What can I do for you, Reis?" She sounded harassed, but Reis pressed forward, knowing this was no social call.

"The suspect in the art gallery bombing is dead," Reis said. "His name is Ash Ferguson, age thirty, no fixed address. You can collect the body at my old apartment."

"You knew the suspect? You should have called me. We could have taken him in."

"He wouldn't have let you take him in." Reis swallowed, trying to hide the emotion in their voice. Now wasn't the time to get sentimental.

"We just picked up Tony Anvas and his associates. Our experts were able to figure out his location from a wall he hadn't quite covered in his video broadcast. That kind of brick is only found in the Glass Pyramid's basement—they had to use a special kind of stone to build the foundation for the heavy glass structure."

"The Killing Committee was operating out of the basement of the seat of government?" Reis gasped. "How did they pull it off underneath so many Kasyovan representatives' noses?"

"We picked up twelve people, all high-ranking officials, bureaucrats, businessmen, and elected representatives. This is going to be the trial of the century, Reis. It's all over."

"No, it's not." Reis thought back to the original Killing Game video. "There were thirteen people around the table. Someone's missing—and I think I know who and why."

"Reis, slow down. There's a lot to unpack here. We're going to have to file a lot of charges today, and undoubtedly some of these people will slip through and walk free. Meanwhile, rioting has started. Anverites are claiming the arrests are politically motivated, that the attack was a Kasyovan setup to frame Anver representatives and force them out of the Assembly. Kasyovans are fighting back, claiming Anver's instability has finally spread to Kasyova."

"Maybe it's time to hold a press conference. If they know Edgar is alive and I'm innocent, maybe it will calm things down," Reis suggested.

"I'll set it up. Reis, I have to go. I'll be in touch with a time and place."

"That's fine. There's something I have to do, first."

"Don't take too long, Reis. We're almost out of time. Having the Committee in custody means nothing if war breaks out. They'll be seen as political prisoners."

Reis hung up. They walked out into the corridor, leaving Ash's body for the Bureau. They had to find Edgar. They were relieved when Edgar came stumbling up the stairs, gun case in hand.

"Edgar..." Reis ran to him and pulled him into a tight embrace. "You look awful."

"Is killing always this hard?" Edgar asked.

"Yeah. It gets easier, but that's probably not a good thing." Reis stared into the middle distance, trying not to think of the lives they'd taken. "I'm sorry. If I'd taken the chance when I had it, you wouldn't have blood on your hands now."

"I knew you'd never be able to take the shot. That's why I volunteered, Reis. You try to hide it from the world, but you have a soft heart. I had to do what you couldn't." Edgar pulled back, handing Reis the gun case. "Take this. I don't want to carry it anymore."

Reis took the gun. They weren't sure they wanted it either. "I called Vos. She picked up the Committee in the basement of the Pyramid."

"Seriously? They were that brazen?" Edgar balked. "How far up does this conspiracy go?"

"Pretty high, from the sound of it. Some of those people will probably be able to wriggle free of their charges, but the immediate threat is over."

"Finally. I need a rest and a shower."

"Not yet. Riots are breaking out. There are still two things left to do. One, we need to hold a press conference. Vos is setting it up. Hopefully, knowing the truth that you're alive and clearing my name will help calm things down a bit. Two, I need to see my father."

"Your father? Isn't he in a nursing home?"

"Yeah. He is." Reis didn't elaborate. "Let's go."

Chapter Twenty-One

EDGAR

The Manor Nursing Home sat on a hill outside of Anver, overlooking the city. Reis stayed silent as they drove. Edgar sat quietly with his thoughts, wondering why Reis had decided to visit the old man now. But if Reis said it was important, he was willing to go along with it. Reis's reasons were usually good ones. Perhaps they needed their father's support after losing Ash. Whatever it took to make them feel better was fine.

Edgar hoped it hadn't opened a chasm between them. He'd taken the shot because he'd had no other choice. Reis hadn't chastised him for it, and yet, they were completely silent, their eyes fixed on the road with no way for Edgar to tell what they were feeling. Would they ever look at him with loving eyes again, or would they always see Ash's killer when they saw Edgar's face?

Had they come so far, defeated such impossible odds, only to see their love wither and die in the end?

Reis pulled into the garage beneath the building and parked the car. They turned off the engine and handed the keys to Edgar, along with their phone.

"I won't be too long. If Vos messages my phone, feel free to respond." Reis got out of the car, leaving Edgar alone with his thoughts.

*

REIS

Reis stepped into the nursing home. The stark white corridors were offset with a multitude of gardens and outdoor spaces, mitigating the sterile environment of the facility. Comfort was what good money bought, and Elias Torell had a lot of it. The Twin City-States had awarded him the Medal of Courage, which gave him a generous stipend from the government each month. He could afford to spend his final days in a manner befitting the hero of Unification.

If he was. Reis felt uncertainty tugging at their spirit. Ash's words burrowed into them like a drill. Had their ex-partner been fucking with them? It was certainly a possibility, but why? Why waste his last words on mocking Reis like he'd won?

Reis reached their dad's room. They gently dismissed the nurse, who set lunch on a tray table and left, closing the door to Elias's room behind her. The room was comfortable, more like a hotel suite than a hospital room. Elias looked thin and frail, but those same soldier's eyes remained firm. Reis wondered how lucid he would be today.

Or was it all an act? Had their father been pulling strings behind the scenes this whole time, pretending to be losing his memories while tearing the foundations out from everything he'd built? It barely seemed possible, looking at him. He absently stirred his dessert into his potatoes, making a sickening soup.

"Dad, don't do that." Reis pulled his fork away. They took the plastic knife, carved up the steak, and fed their father a cube. Their father spit it out.

"Tastes like blood. Who are you, anyway? A new nurse? I liked the other one."

"Dad, it's me. Reis. Your child." Reis closed their eyes, holding back tears. Of course, Ash had been fucking with them. He knew Reis hated to see their proud, heroic father in this state. What better way to punish them than to send them here with false accusations of Elias being somehow involved in the conspiracy? The thirteenth person could be anybody—it easily could have been Ash himself, though Reis suspected he'd been nothing more than a lackey. In a conspiracy of high-ranking officials, Ash was a nobody. He'd never earn a seat on the Committee no matter how many symbols he set alight. He was nothing more than a tool to be used, easily manipulated by his thirst for blood and notoriety.

"Reis. Oh, okay. Reis. Yeah, I remember. I gave you a different name."

"Dad, please—" Panic rose in Reis's gut. They didn't want to hear that name. Not now. Not ever again.

"It's okay. I'm not going to say it." There was a sparkle in his eyes for a brief glimmer of a second, a hint of the man Reis had known. That was the hardest pill to swallow, knowing Elias was in there somewhere, the man who had done his best to raise them, despite knowing nothing beyond being a soldier for a cause.

"Do the terms 'Killing Game' or 'Killing Committee' mean anything to you, Dad?" Reis hated asking. Hated sitting here, still somewhere deep down suspecting their own fragile, forgetful father, even though he was clearly incapable of masterminding so much as his lunch.

"Why would you ask a question like that?"

"Ash said—"

"Oh, Ash! I remember Ash. You ever going to marry that son of a bitch?"

"Ash and I broke up a while back, Dad." Reis struggled to stay calm. They were wasting time, here. They needed to be at the press conference before it was too late to diffuse the tension that was threatening to tear the Twin City-States apart. "I'm with someone else, now. His name is Edgar. Edgar Tobias. He's Kasyovan."

"Like your mother."

"Right!"

"I've heard that name. Where have I heard that name, Reis?"

"He was on the news." Reis decided to skip over the ugly parts where the media claimed Reis was his killer. It wasn't like Elias would remember, anyway. "The Killing Committee was offering a bounty to hunt him down, because he's the son of a famous soul duo. So, I protected him."

"That seems like a noble thing to do." Elias tapped the remote, and the television in the corner sprang to life. Reis hoped the arrests would be on the news, and not Edgar's killing, or their father was just as likely to call for help as hold a conversation with them.

Elias's face paled. "They're arresting patriots, Reis. You can't let them arrest patriots."

"They're no patriots, Dad," Reis explained. "They were involved in a conspiracy to destroy Unification. To split the Twin City-States apart. They wanted to leave your legacy in ruins. The peace you built."

Elias smiled, a wan, distant smile. A knowing smirk. "Oh, Reis. You didn't think Unification was built to last, did you?"

"What?" Reis turned to stare at their father in horror. "What do you mean?" It couldn't be true. Elias Torell couldn't be involved in the conspiracy. He couldn't.

"I opened the gates to Kasyova because we had no other choice. Without them, the anarchy Anver was falling into would have torn the city apart until nothing was left."

"I know that." Reis bit their lip, wondering how much they'd get out of their father before he lost his train of thought.

"We can't be invaded by a foreign power forever. Our differences are too great, our priorities misaligned. I put together a plan, so after ten years Anver would get out of this mess and break out on our own. We got what we needed, Reis. It's time to cut loose. That's why I have this strategy. He's in charge of executing the plan I created, Reis." Elias pointed to the image of Tony Anvas on the screen. "It'll start with killings. He'll kill famous people and start setting Kasyovans and Anverites against one another. The war that will begin will end Unification. Anverites will find purpose in the war. They'll have goals again. They won't drift aimlessly, like you have drifted. They'll have a purpose—Anver's independence. They'll rebuild Anver twice as strong, bathed in the blood of our enemies. They won't fail to rule like last time because they'll be united against a common enemy."

"You planned this all along?" Despair overwhelmed Reis, and their voice left them in a hoarse whisper, the faith ripped from their chest like their father had reached in and torn out Reis's heart. "How could you? You were my *hero*, Dad." Tears streaked Reis's face, falling unbidden. "How can you say "our enemies" with a straight face when Mom was Kasyovan? How can you start a war when she was killed by the last one?"

"Oh, the flower girl! She was pretty, wasn't she? Oh, how we danced!"

"Answer me!" Reis yelled.

"Why are you yelling, Reis?" Elias scratched his head. "I'm confused."

"You told me you planned to start a war with Kasyova all along. Why? I thought you loved Mom."

"It's not personal. War is never personal. It's a means to an end, child. Don't look so angry and hurt. The world isn't all about you, you know. What's that saying...? My mind is hazy. Oh, I know. 'Sometimes you have to break a few eggs to make an omelet.' Is that it?"

Reis stared at their father, as if seeing him for the first time. They closed their eyes, fighting the urge to reach for the pistol still tucked in their waistband. No, killing him would serve no purpose. He was already serving his sentence for crimes against the state, trapped in a broken body and mind that would forever replay and then forget moments from his life. He'd been the architect of Unification and the mastermind behind its destruction, but only the former would come to pass.

Reis balled their hands into fists, determination flooding into their veins. There was no further reason to remain here. Elias Torell had been the thirteenth member of the Killing Committee, or rather, the first, but in his state, he was no longer the man behind the curtain. He'd directed Tony Anvas and the others to carry out his plan, and they had failed.

Or had they? If Reis didn't diffuse the tension between the Twin City-States soon, the Committee could end up winning after all. An independent Anver government would release them all from jail in a heartbeat, their crimes against humanity forgotten. They marched to the door and took one last look behind them at their father mashing the steak cubes in with the dessert and mashed potato while staring absently at the television.

"Where are you going?" Elias asked.

"I'm going to save the Twin City-States and preserve Unification. You're wrong, Dad, and your legacy of war and hate will die with you. We don't need war, fear, or killing to define our purpose. We need one another. That's what I didn't understand before, and what I know now. Thanks for your final lesson, Dad." Reis left the room, wiping their eyes with their sleeve. They looked down, noticing spatters of Ash's blood on their shirt. They zipped up their jacket to hide the stain, walking past the bewildered nurse who rushed into Elias's room to check on him.

Reis marched from the facility with confidence and smiled to see Edgar sitting in the car, waiting for them. They opened the door and sat in the driver's seat.

"Vos called. Press conference is at three, Bureau press room. Are you all right, Reis?"

"No, but I will be." Reis closed their eyes for a moment. "Dad was behind all of it. The Killing Game, the conspiracy to destroy Unification... He planned it all ten years ago. By his twisted logic, the war with Kasyova would unite Anver against a common enemy, giving us a chance to form a government that wasn't divided up into factions like last time."

"At what cost?" Edgar shook his head. "He would have killed so many, and for what? The chance to stamp Anver's name on a passport?"

"He believed the same thing Ash did: war gives warriors a purpose in life." Reis sighed. "He's wrong. A warrior doesn't have to be a killer. A warrior can choose to protect those they love and stand up for peace. That's the path I'm going to choose, Edgar." Reis looked deep into Edgar's eyes, sensing warmth and understanding there. "Let's save the Twin City-States together and end this conflict once and for all."

Chapter Twenty-Two

EDGAR

Vos stood behind the curtain, awaiting their arrival. Edgar held Reis's hand as they hurried through. Vos ushered them onto the podium and Edgar led the way to a chorus of gasps and camera flashes as the media realized they were witnessing a dead man walking. Edgar and Reis took their seats in the middle of the table, and Vos took a spot next to Reis. A couple of other agents assigned to the case filled the other seats, possibly as bodyguards.

"As you can see, rumors of my death have been greatly exaggerated," Edgar said, breaking into nervous laughter. "Reis Asher didn't murder me. The video and crime scene were staged by an agent working with the Killing Committee conspiracy, to sow discord between Anver and Kasyova. Reis—Reis saved my life. They protected me from a plot to kill the children of famous Kasyovans in order to blame Anver and destabilize Unification."

The room erupted into questions. Vos took charge, calling on a journalist sitting in the front row. "Is it true you killed Ash Ferguson, the suspected bomber in the terrorist attack this morning?"

"That—that's correct," Edgar confirmed. "I did what I had to do to protect this country and the lives of its civilians. I make no apology for it."

"Would you say Reis is a hero?"

"I think heroes don't exist," Edgar chimed in. The truth about Elias Torell hadn't come out, not yet, but it undoubtedly would at the conspiracy trial, as the accused tried to pass the blame and slip free of the charges of high treason leveled against them. "I think we're all human, susceptible to the same graces and failings as anybody else."

"Are you romantically involved?"

Reis smiled. Edgar looked over at them, shaking his head, thinking the same thought that was probably running through Reis's head: *a plot to destroy the nation has been revealed, and they want to know if we're in love?*

"That's true," Reis confirmed. "For weeks, the whole nation believed I was his killer, and I was the only one who knew it could never be true."

From there, the room was putty in their hands. They answered hours of questions on the conspiracy, on their flight from the Killing Game, everything they were allowed to say without compromising the trial. Reis had gone from villain of the week to media darling, and they seemed comfortable in the spotlight, even as sadness twinkled in their eyes. Their father's betrayal would hurt for a long time, Edgar realized. It was over now, and they could heal, but the wounds were many, and it would take them both a long time to stop looking over their shoulders.

"I want the Twin City-States to come together," Reis said. "We're not so different. My mother was Kasyovan. She's not as famous as my father, of course, but she ran a florist shop during the civil war. She was killed when shelling destroyed our home. I don't want us to ever fight again. A war between Anver and Kasyova would not be a war for independence, but another dirty civil war, pitting families against one another and putting friends at odds. Yes, Anver and Kasyova have different priorities, but our differences are our strength. We compensate for one another's weaknesses, and we're stronger together." Reis stood. "I want us to come together and sing the anthem of the Twin City-States, and I want us to think of today not as a day where treason almost destroyed us, but a day when we came together and renewed our marriage. Let's think of this as Reunification Day." The national anthem sounded, and everyone stood, placing their hands over their hearts.

Edgar reached for Reis's hand and their fingers entwined, bonding two famous figures of Anver and Kasyova together. With tears in their eyes, they sang a song of peace and unity that echoed around the world.

*

EDGAR

The nationwide vigil of peace and mourning for the victims of the terrorist attack went on throughout the night, as Reis and Edgar arrived at Edgar's apartment under police escort. Edgar unlocked his door, expecting to see his things gone, but they remained exactly as he'd left them that fateful morning when he'd followed Chris into the basement.

"Nice place." Reis slipped off their jacket, revealing the bloodstain underneath. "I need to shower and change, if you don't mind."

"Be my guest," Edgar said. He sat down at his desk, booted his computer, and groaned at the number of mails in his inbox. He'd managed to contact some of his clients in the few moments he'd had a computer, but others—somehow oblivious to the fact he was now *that* Edgar Tobias they were seeing on the news—were quite angry about work he hadn't completed. He fought the urge to shoot off sarcastic e-mails detailing his time dodging attempts on his life. He'd have to try to salvage some of those professional relationships if he wanted to keep on freelancing, and an off-the-cuff remark made when he was tired and nervous wasn't the way to do it.

Reis seemed to take forever in the shower, and Edgar wondered if it was an open invite to join them, but he couldn't assume anything. They hadn't had the chance to sit and talk since he'd shot Ash, and it was long overdue. The fact Reis had held his hand at the press conference and told the media they were a couple was a promising sign, but all Edgar could see in his mind was the bullet shattering Ash's chest, over and over again. His handiwork had killed someone Reis loved, and they'd have to deal with the fallout in due course. They were going to need a lot of therapy before they could even begin to figure out where they were headed from here.

But it all began with talking. Edgar relaxed a little when Reis emerged in the clothes Edgar had laid out for them. They were all huge and far too baggy, of course, but they'd shop for something more suitable later on. Once they'd had time to sleep and figure out what lay ahead.

"You next," Reis said. Edgar shook his head, but Reis insisted, and so Edgar found himself washing away the sweat and tears that had built up on his skin. The warm water felt good, and Edgar smirked as he realized he had hot water and wouldn't have to call maintenance for once. He'd have to find out what had happened to Chris—that was going to be an awkward conversation, for sure, and he chuckled at the thought of it. The world had been turned on its head, and now things were right way up they seemed to make even *less* sense.

Putting on a pair of familiar, clean jeans felt like heaven, though, and he decided to take delight in the small things and leave the rest for later. He emerged from the bedroom and sat on the couch next to Reis.

"So, where do we go from here, Reis? I'll understand if you don't want to see my face again after today. I took the life of someone you cared about."

"Ash killed a lot of people. I think it was death he was chasing. I don't want you to carry it around with you. I'm not going to hold it against you. In the end, you saved my life. He *would* have shot me—of that I have no doubt."

Edgar nodded. "I will carry it, probably for the rest of my life."

"That's fair. I don't suppose I'll ever forget the mercenaries in the greenhouse, or Grady dying before my eyes."

"Are you going to be okay, Reis?"

"In time. I think my father's betrayal was hardest to bear. You were right when you said there are no heroes, only humans. I learned that lesson today."

"You couldn't have known."

"The Killing Game killed so many people before they targeted you. I can't help but wonder if there was something I could have done if I'd only paid more attention." Reis sighed. "It doesn't matter now. It's all over. We're safe. We made it. The Twin City-States live to see another day."

"Not just another day. A new era. You should go into politics, Reis. That speech was something else."

"I'm too honest for politics." Reis smiled. "They would cut me to shreds. I guess Dad and Ash were right about one thing—this conflict did give me a sense of purpose. I was aimless, meandering through life. Now I think I know what I want to do."

"You were talking with Vos a lot after the meeting. Did something come up?"

"The Political Crimes division is massively understaffed to deal with a trial of this magnitude. I can't work on the case, for obvious reasons, but Vos says there are plenty of openings and my help would be welcomed, especially after I was able to think on my feet and track down Ash."

"Is that something you'd like to do?" Edgar asked.

"Yeah, I think so. I want to protect this country. What better way than to uphold order and the rule of law? Besides, I need a little bit of excitement now and then."

"If Vos sold you on thrills, she's a liar. I'm going to imagine you'll spend most of your days behind a desk, dealing with paperwork."

"I'm sure that's true," Reis said. "There's a lot of training I'll have to go through too. One doesn't just walk into the Bureau, regardless of the recommendations. I'll probably have to enroll in a four-year college, for starters. It's a career path, but it's more direction than I've had in a long time."

"Where do I fit into all this?" Edgar asked. He drummed his fingers on the couch, nervous as hell. What if Reis's new direction didn't involve him?

"I'd like you to keep being you." Reis smiled. "You came to Anver to write computer programs, so if that's what you want to do, I want you to keep going. I'd like to keep seeing you—if it's okay. I'm not ready to pop the question yet, but we have something good together, Edgar. If you're willing, I want to see where it goes."

"I'm more than willing." Edgar's fears faded away, his gut finally settling. He pulled Reis close and kissed them, the time for words passing by as their lips locked. They could talk more in the morning. For now, what they needed was sleep, and lots of it.

Epilogue

Four years later

"Does it suit me?" Reis stood looking in the mirror, admiring the casual suit they'd had tailored for their job at the Bureau. Their ID hung around their neck on a lanyard, clashing with the slick blue tie Reis had picked out for their first day on the job, but they were willing to go along with it.

"You look stunning," Edgar said. "You'll knock 'em dead with that smile."

"That would make my job a lot easier." Reis's fingers went to the gun in its holster at their side. It had taken a lot of therapy and nightmares to get through the psychological effects of the Killing Game, and it had left its mark on both of them. Far from pushing them apart, they'd only come closer because of it. They'd shared an experience few others could understand, and shared their grief, pain, and anxiety when it surfaced.

The television blared from the other room. Tony Anvas and the other Committee members had been sentenced to life in jail, at the culmination of a year-long trial in which hundreds of witnesses had testified, including Reis and Edgar. The evidence had been overwhelming, and the treason charges had stuck. Popular opinion had lampooned them as villains, but Reis still remembered how close they'd come to all-out war.

Elias Torell had died before he could be called to the stand. The other players had revealed him as the origin of the Killing Game. His reputation had tarnished somewhat, but Reis had been spared the pain of a court deciding whether their father was fit enough to stand trial. He'd died in his sleep, and it had been a relief, more than anything. Reis had never been back to see him after he'd revealed he was the originator of the plot against the Twin City-States. It had taken a lot of therapy to work though Reis's disgust and betrayal, but Reis was finally getting there.

"We've come a long way," Reis said. "I didn't know if we would make it, but I'm glad we did. This life... If I hadn't decided to protect you when I saw you being attacked by some guy with a crowbar, I might still be sitting in my apartment, wondering where my life was going."

Edgar put his hands on Reis's shoulders. "I'm glad you did, or I wouldn't be alive." He'd thanked Reis a million times, but a life was a debt that could never be repaid, not really. Still, Edgar enjoyed lavishing his love and pride onto Reis whenever possible, to Reis's chagrin. "I'm proud of you." He kissed Reis's neck.

"Stop it, or I'll have to get undressed, and we don't have time for that." Reis batted Edgar's hands away, desire obvious in their stare. "I can't be late on my first proper day." They'd been training concurrently with their degree, which had been paid for out of the million in cryptocurrency which still sat in Reis's online wallet. It was the closest to compensation they were going to get for the trouble the Killing Committee had put them through, though they were always reluctant to spend what they saw as "blood money."

"Good luck," Edgar said, kissing Reis full on the lips. They lingered, savoring the moment. Even now, four years later, they struggled to break the habit of thinking every kiss might be their last. Perhaps it was for the best. They couldn't take each other for granted that way.

"I love you," Reis said, waving as they turned and walked out the front door to where a shiny black Bureau car waited for them.

"I love you too," Edgar called after them. He watched the car pull out and closed the door. He padded over to the computer, where a small mountain of freelance coding jobs was piling up in his inbox. He sighed, pouring himself another cup of coffee, as he glanced up at the news one more time. A chill ran over his spine, as it did several times a day, when he thought how easily he could be six feet under. Instead, he was planning to get through some work and invite Teon and Sebastian over for dinner. He switched the channel, tired of seeing Tony Anvas's unrepentant face. A commercial popped up for The Soulmates' greatest hits CD, and he smiled as he heard a clip of "Everything But The Son." The warm voices of his fathers soothed his spirit, and Edgar sat down at his desk to begin another day in the paradise of peace he and Reis had fought for and won.

About Reis Asher

Reis Asher (he/him) is a transmasculine author living in rural Pennsylvania with his husband and four cats. He loves video games, reading, technology, and of course, writing.

He enjoys shining a spotlight on queer characters and their adventures in a diverse range of worlds, from the fantastical to the everyday.

Catch him on Twitter where he's happy to interact.

Email
landale@me.com

Twitter
@landale

Also from NineStar Press

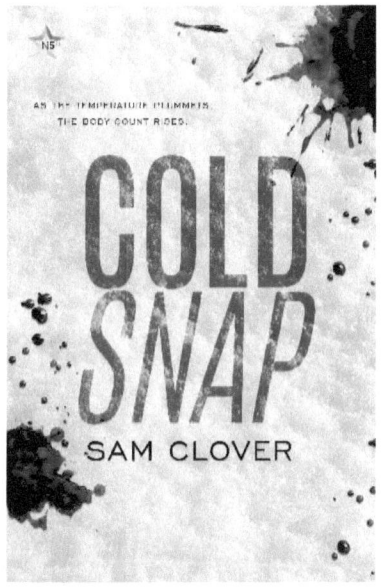

Cold Snap by Sam Clover

A lifetime of bad experiences has left Iddy homeless and wary of shelters.

Rumors of a monster hunting the city streets at night surface, but between the cold and predators of the human variety, Iddy has more important things to worry about. That is until he comes face-to-face with the monster and survives. Now, it has him in its sights.

Birthday Presents by Dianne Hartsock

Crimson loves to dance. He adores watching the pretty boys grind to the frantic beat of the music and picking out his lover for the evening. But more than that, he lives for his birthday, that one day a year he gives into his darker impulses: choosing a young man to lure into the alleyway with promises of sex, then slitting his throat in the midst of their passion and reveling in the hot blood on his hands.

For Tracey Winston, life has become a nightmare. Kidnapped from a nightclub in Boulder, Colorado, brutalized and raped by Crimson, he's held captive in a cabin in the Rocky Mountains along with sweet Kyle, a young man Crimson keeps chained to his bed and is slowly torturing to death. Though Tracey manages to escape with Kyle's help, he has to leave Kyle behind in Crimson's cruel hands.

Detective Gene Mallory has never stopped looking for his brother Kyle, kidnapped from a nightclub seven months previously. The case breaks open when Tracey Winston comes forth at the urging of his new boyfriend, claiming to have knowledge of where Crimson is hiding out. A manhunt begins with Crimson continuously slipping through their net. Lives are on the line, with both Gene and Tracey being targeted by the killer. A traitor in their midst tips Crimson off to their plans.

Crimson's birthday has come and gone, and he will kill again.

Third Eye by Rick R. Reed

Who knew that a summer thunderstorm and a lost little boy would conspire to change single dad Cayce D'Amico's life in an instant? With Luke missing, Cayce ventures into the woods near their house to find his son, only to have lightning strike a tree near him, sending a branch down on his head. When he awakens the next day in the hospital, he discovers he has been blessed or cursed—he isn't sure which—with psychic ability. Along with unfathomable glimpses into the lives of those around him, he's getting visions of a missing teenage girl.

When a second girl disappears soon after the first, Cayce realizes his visions are leading him to their grisly fates.

Cayce wants to help, but no one believes him. The police are suspicious. The press wants to exploit him. And the girls' parents have mixed feelings about the young man with the "third eye."

Cayce turns to local reporter Dave Newton and, while searching for clues to the string of disappearances and possible murders, a spark ignites between them. Little do they know that nearby, another couple—dark and murderous—are plotting more crimes and wondering how to silence the man who knows too much about them.

Connect with NineStar Press

www.ninestarpress.com

www.facebook.com/ninestarpress

www.facebook.com/groups/NineStarNiche

www.twitter.com/ninestarpress

www.instagram.com/ninestarpress